THE FINAL RAVEN

To Elizabeth,

Finian Black

Best wishes,

Finian Black

Weybourne Press

This edition published by Weybourne Press 2017

Visit the author's website at www.finianblack.com
Follow the author on Twitter @finianblack
Email the author at finian.black@gmail.com

ISBN-13: 978-1546786917
ISBN-10: 1546786910

FOR SARA

1

Just as night followed day the ravens were always there, guarding the Tower of London. Sergeant Major Sam McKenna shivered and pulled his cloak tightly around his shoulders. The frost was already thick on the ground as the last visitors made their way past the Bloody Tower and Water Lane. The Christmas trees glittered. A flake or two of snow drifted down. Just one family remained on the edge of Tower Green. McKenna wandered over to them.

'Look, dad,' said the boy, who was no more than seven or eight. He was pointing at a few enormous black birds fluttering their wings and clacking their beaks. 'The ravens are coming closer.'

'It's because they're hungry,' McKenna said. The family turned to see who had spoken. The boy's eyes widened.

'Are you a real Beefeater?' he asked.

McKenna smiled.

'Our full title is Yeoman Warder of Her Majesty's Royal Palace and Fortress and a member of the Sovereign's Body Guard of the Yeoman Guard Extraordinary, but everybody calls us Beefeaters.'

He kneeled down next to the boy.

'An old legend says that if there are no ravens at the Tower, Britain will fall. They're here to look after us and so we look after them.' He held up a tablet. Seven green bars flickered across the screen. 'Each bird has a microchip implanted into it. We can keep track of their vital signs to make sure they're healthy. Amazing what you can do with technology, eh?'

The boy nodded.

'So, time to lead them in for their tea. I'm known as the Ravenmaster, although I reckon they're the ones in charge and I just do what they want me to. You can walk with them if you like.'

He glanced at the ravens, making sure they were playing the game. It wouldn't do for them all to hop off in the opposite direction.

'What's the matter with that one?' the boy asked.

McKenna hesitated. One of the ravens was staggering a little. Its wings were dragging in the frost. The bird's beak opened slightly. A single drop of blood fell from it. As the Ravenmaster and the family watched, the raven keeled over and lay on its side, gasping for air.

Fighting for life.

2

Luca Broom gazed up at a huge round table.

'And there you can see the image of Henry the Eighth,' droned the tour guide, a dull little man with a nasally voice. 'He ordered that he was painted as King Arthur surrounded by his knights. He wanted his Tudor family to be as important as the Plantagenets who had come before him.'

The history lesson about the table continued, but only Luca was paying any attention. He closed his eyes to block out the chatter of his classmates and tried to concentrate on what the man was saying.

'Of course, King Arthur never really existed. Neither did his castle, Camelot, nor his sword Excalibur. And certainly not the wizard Merlin, who pops up in the old stories. But the old kings believed in it all so they made sure their people did too. As I've said, the table has hung here in Winchester for centuries, since the Wars of the Roses and the Black Death.'

The guide's voice rose for dramatic effect.

'Like the London bird plague they're talking about on the news, eh?'

He laughed nervously but the joke wasn't funny, not when it was rumoured that two out of every three people infected were dying.

'Thank you,' interrupted their teacher. 'I'm not sure I want my year nine class to be thinking about that. Perhaps we should move on.'

'Oh, okay,' said the guide. 'I didn't mean to scare anybody. Always good to bring history up to date, yes?'

Luca's head suddenly buzzed with a familiar noise, like hundreds of bees flitting in a jar. He knew what would come next. Even though his eyes were still closed, he saw massive black birds with beaks as big as swords. Then he saw a tower, just visible through dark mist, and a young girl with red hair. As quickly as they had come, the images and buzzing sound were gone.

'Watch it, Broom,' said the boy next to him as Luca staggered sideways.

'Sorry.'

He wondered, not for the first time in the last two weeks, if he was going mad. What other reason was there for him to keep seeing things that weren't really there?

A phone pinged off to Luca's right. Then another, and another. The guide frowned.

'Please keep your mobiles turned off.'

Nobody paid him any attention. More phones were pinging.

'It's from my dad. He says I've got to get home. The plague's not just in London any more.'

'Same. Some people are sick in Southampton. Man, that's way too close.'

4

'We're going to Wales. My uncle's got a place in the mountains.'

More pings. More texts. The guide's hands were waving, trying to restore order. Luca's phone buzzed in his pocket.

LUCA - STAY AWAY. GET OUT OF TOWN. I'M SORRY. I LOVE YOU AND DAD LOVED YOU. X

Then the lights went out and the hall was filled with screams and shouts in the sudden unexpected darkness. A fist rammed against Luca's arm. He pushed it away, all his senses fired. Sparks cascaded down the wall, lighting it up like a firework display.

'Look at that!' someone shouted.

The table was splitting, first in a thin white line of light that shivered around the top, then quickly ripping apart from top to bottom, tearing like wet paper rather than solid oak. Luca stared in horror at what was happening. Seemingly from nowhere, thousands of birds cascaded out of the destroyed table, flying around in panicked circles. Some fell to the floor, their wings flapping uselessly, their beaks dripping blood.

Luca backed away, his mind racing. He had seen the tower and the girl. He had seen birds. Now this. Something seriously weird was going on.

'Get out of here!' his teacher called.

Luca didn't need telling twice. He sprinted for the door, ignoring the crunch of the fragile birds under his feet. The doorway was quickly jammed with struggling bodies and flailing birds. Luca shoved hard against them, his legs pinned, his chest squeezed. He managed a gulp of air and then he pushed even harder. The weight was building against him. Lights danced across his vision. Then, with seconds to go until he lost consciousness, he shot out like a cork from a bottle. He scrambled to his feet, coughing painfully.

What the hell just happened?

He was running on instinct, heading for home. Winchester was deserted - no cars, shop lights flicking off as he passed. Something bad had clearly happened whilst his class was in the hall. He heard a siren, then another. A shadow passed over him, an instant night. The sky was dark with screeching birds.

Luca slid into a doorway. He called his mum's number. No reply. He texted, then called again, panic rising. The plague was still just in London, according to last night's news. Just a few cases. Carry on as normal. No need to worry. Well, that was obviously a load of rubbish. And nobody had said anything about the crazy stuff he had just witnessed.

He needed to know what her message meant. She had mentioned his dad...she never did that. Never.

He checked the sky. All clear, the birds gone to who the hell knew where. He ran on, picking up speed. If his mum was ill, she wasn't going to a hospital full of dead people. He would take her somewhere quiet and wait for her to get better. She would be the one out of three - she would live. As he rounded the last corner, he cursed and skidded back out of sight. There were two patrol cars and an ambulance parked up outside his flat. A police officer in white protective overalls and a gas mask marched towards him.

'You're coming with us, son,' the officer rasped through his respirator. 'The whole area's being evacuated.'

Luca sprinted towards his front door. Two more officers cut him off. Luca changed direction, heading away from home. He had to find a way of getting in, but first he had to avoid being caught and dragged away.

'Stop!'

Luca ignored the order and kept running. He wouldn't be able to help his mum from the back of a police car. After a few minutes he slowed down, out of breath. Then he slammed into a broad chest.

'Nice try,' the officer said, pinning Luca's arms to his sides, 'but I was running around these streets before you were even born. I took a short cut when I saw you leg it.'

Luca kicked and fought but it was no good. The man's grip was too strong. He leaned in close. Condensation clouded the inside of his mask as he spoke.

'Nobody's going to hurt you, son. Calm down. You just need to come with me and we'll get you to a safe place.'

Luca was just about to tell him exactly what he thought of that idea when everything turned bright red. A flash blinded him, rapidly followed by a deafening boom that flung him onto the ground. The officer was screaming. Just then, he heard a deep roar and a weird scraping noise which sounded horribly like claws. Luca saw a huge blurred shape in front of him. He tried to make out what it was but his eyes were still refusing to fully co-operate.

'No!' the officer yelled, his voice full of terror. 'Please don't hurt me!'

Luca's eyes cleared. He almost wished they hadn't.

'That can't be a bear,' he whispered.

But it was. A real live brown bear, up on its hind legs. The creature's eyes were black pools. Drool splashed from its jaws. The bear threw back its head and roared. It was too much for the officer. He turned and ran. The bear roared again and started to change shape. The thick fur melted away. It only took a few seconds for the creature to disappear and a man stood there instead. He was tough-looking, his face lined and weathered. He wore a thick overcoat, boots and jeans. His close-cropped hair was mainly grey. An ugly leaden gargoyle hung around his neck. The man waved and for a moment, Luca's confused brain saw the hand as something else – an enormous paw.

'Sorry if I scared you,' the man said. 'Right, let's get out of here before anybody else comes along and sees us.'

The man clicked his fingers and everything went black.

***

Impossibly, Luca and the man were in his mum's tiny bedroom, staring into her feverish eyes.

'Mum!'

She did not respond.

'We're here and not here at the same time,' the man said. 'You're just a shadow. Even so, she can see you if you really want her to.'

His hand rested on Luca's shoulder.

'The plague virus is spreading through her. I'm sorry you have to watch it.'

Luca angrily shrugged away the man's hand.

'Mum,' he said once more. 'I'm here.'

Her eyes cleared and a faint smile spread across her pale face. Luca was frozen, focused on mum, willing her to see him properly. She nodded weakly, then looked behind him.

'You,' she snarled.

'Yes,' the man replied. 'I told you this day would come.'

'You did.' She closed her eyes. 'I texted him. Told him to get away.'

'He can't escape who he is. You know that.'

Luca's mum slumped back.

'You look after my boy.'

'I'll do what I can.'

Luca couldn't speak, his mouth was so dry.

'You're going to have to trust him, my darling,' his mum said. 'Take this and keep it safe.'

Her hand emerged from under the duvet. She held out a tattered photograph.

'I remember that,' Luca whispered.

It had been taken eight years before. He was a child of six in his mum's arms. Dad was dressed in his desert combats, ready to fly away to Afghanistan, to a war from which he never returned.

'We always knew,' she croaked.

Luca's fingers trembled as he took the photograph.

'Knew what? You've never shown me this before. I don't understand.'

She coughed, and it was horrible to see her beautiful face etched with pain.

'Hold my hand,' Luca said. 'Come with me!'

'I can't. I love you.'

His mum looked away. The man touched Luca's shoulder again.

'Time to go.'

3

On the sixty fifth floor of the Shard, Gwendoline Madoc snuggled into her thick coat and stared down at London, spread out like her own private monopoly board.

So, she thought, I'm stuck in here with nothing to do and nowhere to go, just because of some stupid virus.

What were they calling it on the news? Bird plague? Like something from a bad film. What a rubbish fourteenth birthday this was turning out to be.

Gwen shivered in the freezing wind as snowflakes tossed around her face. A thin pigeon landed on the balcony. It swayed unsteadily, trying to flap its sodden wings. Then it pitched forwards, a bead of dark blood leaking from its beak. She squirmed away from the twitching corpse.

That is so disgusting, she thought, utterly horrified.

Another thought wormed into her brain.

It must have the plague.

She ran inside the sprawling apartment and dropped into a sofa that could easily seat eight people but had never needed to. That could only happen if Gwen had any friends to invite over for movies and gossip like a normal teenager might do, but the daughter of the world's most powerful media magnate could never be described as normal. She understood that only too well.

The whole of the wall behind her was covered with television screens, all beaming their message into the homes of the millions who subscribed to her father's cable networks. The presenters spoke English, French, Spanish, Gujarati, Japanese and many more languages besides. Wherever you went in the world the television you watched was brought to you courtesy of Madoc Corporation. And every fifteen minutes a news bulletin changed your opinions and fed them back to you as fact.

Gwen ignored the screens. They were just wallpaper. Other children grew up watching cuddly puppets and cartoons; Gwen knew twenty four seven media.

She checked her watch. Four fifteen. He had promised they would meet at four. Her iPhone rang.

'What is it?'

'Your father wanted me to tell you that he's sorry, miss,' her personal assistant stammered. 'The plague stories need his personal attention. He's had to cancel, but he said he'll make it up with a bigger party and twice as many presents tomorrow.'

'He's had to cancel,' Gwen repeated.

'Yes, miss.'

Gwen thought she heard a nervous gulp.

'No, miss. I mean, yes. I mean, I'm sorry, miss. I really am.'

Gwen closed her eyes. She should have expected something like this. The work always came first, after all. How many times had her father droned on at her about it? We have all this because of hard work, he liked to say. The poor people are lazy. They don't want to drag themselves out of the gutter like he had done, building his empire from nothing so that he could provide this wonderful life for his only child.

'Where is he?'

Her assistant paused.

'I don't know.'

'Yes, you do. Tell me now.'

'I think Mr Madoc's on the way to his office, miss.'

The assistant was in trouble whatever she did.

'I'm sure it will be worth the wait, miss. Mr Madoc has re-arranged everything for tomorrow.'

'He can't actually re-arrange for it to be my birthday tomorrow, can he?'

Gwen ended the call without another word.

His precious news is more important to him than me, she thought, the anger bubbling inside her. But I won't take no for an answer.

Perhaps if he saw how upset she was, he would change his mind. Surely the editors could cope for a few hours. She stared down. A single tear dripped onto the floor. The thought of yet another diamond necklace was too much. She just wanted to feel loved again, just as she had done when her mother was alive.

She pictured the smile on her mother's face, the warmth in her eyes and the sunlight on her long blonde hair. She remembered her laughing at silly things and dancing to cheesy eighties songs. Was it already nearly a year? A single thought overwhelmed everything else.

I miss you.

4

Luca's flat was gone. He was standing in a large circular room with no windows and a high timber ceiling. Stone steps led up the wall to a closed trapdoor. It was dimly lit, and a low humming noise hurt his ears. He reached for his phone but his hand found nothing except the photograph.

'Must have dropped it,' he said to himself.

'Who are you?'

He jumped at the voice, his fists up ready to fight. There were two of them, a boy of about twelve and a girl his own age. In the low light they could have been ghosts but the boy moved towards him and Luca could see he was solid enough.

'I'm Freddie,' the boy said. 'My sister's called Jess. Who are you?'

Luca didn't know what to say or do. His brain wasn't firing properly, as if he was struggling to wake up from the deepest sleep. Everything was fragments of dreams and memories – the great hall with the birds, the police, the bear, the man and his mum...she had known him. She had known what this all meant.

'We were in the hospital,' continued the boy. 'Mum and dad are dead. Josh is sick. That's our little brother. The police wanted us to go with them but we didn't want to. They were scared off by this bear but he was really a man, and now we're here.'

So they saw him as well, thought Luca. The boy's voice was calm, but Luca saw the fear in his eyes. Why wouldn't there be? What had started as a normal day had turned into off the scale insane.

'I think it's just the three of us,' said Jess. 'Perhaps we should wait here for the man to come. He can tell us what's happening.'

You got a phone?' Luca asked.

'No.'

'Well, I'm not staying,' Luca said, looking for a way out. 'You two can do what you like.'

There was door in front of him. That was all he needed. The humming noise was louder and as he pulled the handle, he realised it was the wind building outside.

'Don't open it,' Freddie said, but it was too late.

The humming was now a full blown roar as the wind rushed in. Luca was blown back by a surge of snow that was immediately up to his ankles, piling in like thick porridge. He tried to close the door but the wind was just too strong. His mouth was full of snow and he turned away, choking. The blizzard was in there with them.

'Up the stairs, quick!'

He waded towards the others. They were on the bottom step, which was just about to disappear under the snow. The walls were already coated as it blew around the room. Jess reached out for his hand and pulled him closer. They began to climb.

'It's filling up faster than we can go,' Luca gasped.

He was right. The snow was thick on the steps above them, and it was rising steadily from below, building up in thick drifts with every second that passed. Another huge gust of wind hit them but they just managed to stay upright. At this rate, the whole room would be full in a few minutes.

'We've got to get through the trapdoor.'

'We don't have a key.'

'Then find one!'

'There,' said Jess.

She pointed at a brick where the wall met the ceiling.

'What is it?'

'It's not fixed in. Can you see?'

The brick was sticking out slightly and there was no mortar around it. Luca pulled at it but he couldn't get enough of a grip to work it free. His fingers were throbbing painfully with the biting wind and snow.

'Let me try,' said Freddie.

He pushed past Luca. His smaller fingers seemed to get more traction. He wiggled the brick from side to side.

'It's coming.'

'Hurry up,' Luca said, sounding calmer than he felt.

Freddie grunted, either as an answer or with the effort of freeing the brick. It came loose and he tumbled backwards, disappearing into the snow.

'No!' his sister screamed. She scrambled around, trying to grab him. Luca did the same. The cold was horrendous. His fingers felt like they were on fire, but he kept going. His hand bumped against an ankle and he pulled hard. Freddie slid out of the snow and onto the step, coughing and retching.

'Get the key,' he gasped.

Luca reached into the gap in the wall. If there was nothing there...

'Yes!'

There *was* a key. There were only seconds to go. If the key didn't fit, they would be buried and dead. He slid the key into the keyhole. It turned easily. The trapdoor dropped down and fresh air flooded in. They climbed up into another circular room, this time with windows set high up in the walls. Luca pulled up the trapdoor. They collapsed onto the floor, utterly exhausted.

'We did it,' Luca said.

'We might have to do it again,' Jess replied.

The wind was suddenly stronger. The windows rattled like beans in a can. They weren't going to last long, and already the snow was pushing up through the floorboards.

'I think we've just bought ourselves some time to figure out how we get up there,' said Jess, pointing up at the ceiling.

A rope hung down from another trapdoor, too high to reach.

'Great,' Luca replied. 'What do we do, fly?'

One of the windows gave under the pressure of the wind, blowing glass and snow into the room. It was like being inside an enormous snow globe. Another window exploded. At this rate, it would be just a few minutes before this room was buried like the last.

'We wait for it to fill up,' said Freddie.

Luca stared at him. Had the kid gone mad?

'What?'

'Easy. We wait for the snow to take us up to the rope, then we pull it.'

There was no time left to argue. Two more windows burst and snow cascaded in from all directions. The wind noise was so loud, it was impossible to talk any more. They huddled together under the rope. Luca watched, fascinated, as Freddie lay down on the snow, spreading himself into a star shape.

'What's he doing?' Luca screamed into Jess's ear.

'Making a snow angel. He won't sink if he lies like that.'

'Bloody hell, that's clever.'

'Copy him, then.'

It was crazy, dangerous and utterly brilliant. It took some doing, because the snow blew straight into his eyes and mouth, but once Luca was on the surface, a new calm crept over him. He could feel the massive pressure of the snow underneath him, pushing them up. He wondered if the walls would burst but the building seemed solid enough to take it. They just might get out of this room, but would there be another and then another? How far up would they have to go?

The rope was now only two metres or so away. They were level with the destroyed windows and the mean wind ripped at Luca's face. He was past being cold – his whole body was numb, almost paralysed by the freezing snow that was wrapping him up like a shroud.

Stay awake, he thought. He focused on the rope, swinging above him. He was tempted to stand up and grab it but he knew he would slide under the snow, like slipping into wet concrete. The wind was gone, lost with the shattered windows. They were in a rapidly shrinking tube with nowhere to go but up.

'Who wants to pull the rope?' Freddie asked.

'Help yourself,' Luca replied. 'Just don't miss.'

The snow was building around them even more quickly, banking up and then toppling over like slow motion waves on a beach. Luca fought back the claustrophobia as the gap between them and the ceiling closed. Freddie reached up. He pulled the rope but nothing happened.

'Help me,' he grunted.

Luca heaved with everything he had. Jess did the same. Luca imagined that above them was another room already full of snow, and that when the trapdoor opened they would be engulfed, but he kept pulling all the same because that was the only choice he had.

Then the door gave and a freezing blast of air hit them full in the face. The door wedged against the snow and was immediately half buried.

'Go!'

Luca shoved the others ahead of him and they all scrambled through with seconds to spare. They stood up in a third circular room, but this was made of glass. A narrow door led out onto a stone ledge. Luca winced, ready for the panes to shatter, but the wind wasn't penetrating with any strength.

'This is all crazy,' he muttered.

'Like a man who can turn into a bear?' asked Jess.

'Yeah. That kind of crazy. What is this place?'

'An old lighthouse,' Freddie said. 'The light would have been in here.'

That made sense – circular rooms and a tall tower topped with a glass room.

'Smart thinking,' said Luca. 'Which means we're a long way from the ground.'

'Yep.'

Before Luca had a chance to respond, the wind picked up again, buffeting the glass, rattling them harshly against their frames. Snow continued to swell up through the open trapdoor.

'This room is going to be full in a minute,' Luca said. 'We've had it.'

'So we go out there,' replied Freddie, and he opened the door.

It was as if every jet engine in the world was roaring at the same time. Luca was slammed against the glass. Jess and Freddie were tangled up next to him. The wind pushed them back like a giant's hand. The snow swirled up into a thick choking fog.

Luca knew that unless they got out of there, they would suffocate. He grabbed whatever he could of the others and dragged himself forwards to where he hoped the door was. He had no idea what to do once they were through. Just escaping that space was all that mattered.

'Come on,' he yelled, urging them to do as he was doing. The wind knocked them back and sideways but Luca wasn't going to give up. They had been through too much for that. They were out of the room and on the ledge with nowhere left to go. Luca collapsed onto the slabs and closed his eyes. The madness of it all overtook him. He had nothing left. He was going to die out there in the freezing wind and snow of an impossible lighthouse.

'Look at that.'

Freddie sounded urgent but Luca ignored him. It was over.

'Look!'

'Shut up,' Luca muttered. 'I've had it.'

'No way.'

A hand pulled his chin around.

'What the hell is that?'

A muddy black cloud was approaching at great speed, surging and rumbling. The ground seemed to shift and the whole building shuddered. Then the cloud broke apart into hundreds of individual shapes, each one calling and screaming. As they came closer, Luca saw that they were huge black birds.

'Ravens!' shouted Freddie.

Like in my head, Luca thought, and for a split second he saw the tower and the red haired girl, and the birds that Freddie had said were ravens.

Then they were engulfed by them. The bitterly cold wind was replaced by a warm torrent of air from countless flapping wings. Luca was deafened by their cries. He struggled against them but there was no escape. He might as well have fought to hold back an ocean. Unlike the sickly birds in the great hall, these were powerful and healthy looking animals. Luca gagged on the intense smell, a mixture of old food and ammonia.

Then, unbelievably, crazily, magically, he was carried up into the air by the raven's wings and claws, over the lighthouse and out to sea. Luca flailed his arms. He knocked against a raven's head. The bird turned and nipped his fingers. It glared at him before wheeling away. Luca caught a glimpse of Freddie and Jess nearby.

'We're flying!' Freddie shouted. 'Fantastic!'

Luca struggled frantically but there was no way of escaping. The birds were holding them up and guiding them with definite intent. They were moving in unison, heading along the coast. The snow had cleared. A billion stars arched over them. It was the most terrifying and beautiful thing that Luca had ever seen, hanging in that endless nothingness. And as he punched and kicked out against the birds, a voice whispered in his brain.

Don't fight. Let us carry you home.

The voice was soothing, almost hypnotic. Luca's eyelids sagged. His arms and legs were like lead. He sagged down. The ravens closed in around him, forming an impossibly comfortable feather hammock. He was ready to sleep and perhaps, for just a few seconds, he did.

Then he jolted awake. Something had changed. The ravens were no longer carrying them along gently. They were speeding up and heading down. The children screamed as they plunged over a cliff edge towards the foaming water. Luca braced for the impact, but the ravens swerved and lifted, then through a tiny crack in the cliff face. They were in a tunnel. Luca bumped against the sides, flipping up and over. The ravens were no longer holding him. He fell further and further into darkness and there was nothing he could do. Then it was over. They were on soft warm sand, in a cavern so large it seemed like the sky had followed them in.

5

'Get me the Sydney editor on the line in the next ten seconds or you're on a one-way trip to Siberia, do you understand?' John Madoc roared into the face of his assistant as he swept into his office.

'Yes, sir,' the man whimpered. He almost ran out, leaving Madoc alone in the vast space.

The billionaire sighed and brushed a hand across his ebony hair. He wore a dark blue chalk striped suit, a white monogrammed shirt and a silver tie. His shoes were as black as his hair and nearly as shiny. He examined his nails and frowned. There was the faintest blemish on one finger. The manicurist would be dismissed tomorrow.

Madoc scanned the hundred screens adorning the walls, listening to what was being reported about the spreading bird plague. It was serious once-in-a-lifetime news and it needed to be the headline everywhere. Unfortunately, on the east coast of Australia people were waking to be told that a famous cricketer was getting married to a slightly more famous singer.

The phone rang on his desk. He glanced at his watch. Twelve seconds had passed. Madoc considered whether to act upon his threat.

No, he thought. I'm in a forgiving mood.

He picked up the phone.

'Madoc.'

'Good morning, sir.'

The voice in his ear was tinny and high pitched.

'It's actually the afternoon here,' he replied.

Silence. Madoc imagined the scene in Sydney. He saw the panic on the face of the editor, his staff paralysed, wondering why they were receiving a call from Mr Madoc himself.

'Yes sir. Of course. Good afternoon, sir. How are you?'

'I'm well. Thank you for enquiring. But I would be even better if your idiot newsreader was bothering to mention the bird plague. I would have thought that was more worthy of a headline than...than...'

Madoc struggled to control his temper. He lost the battle.

'...than a celebrity wedding!'

'I'm sorry, sir. I can't apologise enough. The plague story is more important, of course. I'll find out what's going on.'

Madoc sighed.

'No, you won't. You're fired.'

He replaced the phone and sat down at his desk. The clock on the opposite wall said 4:27.

Too late for the party, he told himself. There's too much to do here and all far too important. Better to give Gwendoline my full attention tomorrow.

He made another call.

'Randall, I need you now.'

Almost immediately, a tall man with a thin face entered Madoc's office through a hidden door. The man wore a pale tie and a dark suit. A red lapel pin in the shape of the letter M flashed in the ceiling spotlights.

'You wanted me, Mr Madoc.'

'Yes. Has the Prime Minister replied?'

Gareth Randall, Madoc's most loyal servant for more than twenty years, shook his head.

'Not yet, sir, but I believe he will have to call soon. There are cases of the plague as far north as the Scottish border and reports of dead birds all along the east coast, so it won't be long before the sickness hits right across mainland Britain. The airports and ferry terminals will have to be closed. Britain will be locked down.'

The two men fell silent. The breakfast headline in Sydney was no longer about a celebrity wedding.

'So from release to epidemic in a week. Even quicker than I imagined,' Madoc whispered. 'The Prime Minister will beg me for the vaccine once he understands that every other laboratory is months behind us.'

'Yes, sir.'

Madoc looked up.

'I sense that you have some doubts.'

'No doubts, sir. Just regret that so many people will die.'

'Regret? Weak talk. The population is expendable. They're pawns in the bigger game and you know that. Don't go soft on me, Randall. Not now, when we're so close.'

'No, sir. There is something else you should know. A slight complication. One of my spies in the police has reported a strange event in Winchester. A bear appeared out of nowhere.'

'A bear?'

'Then the creature disappeared just as quickly taking a boy with it.'

'Who's the boy? One of them?'

'Possibly. I'm working to identify him.'

'Magician's work,' growled Madoc.

'Agreed, sir.'

'So he knows.'

'We don't need to worry. Everything is progressing exactly as planned. I will inform you the moment the Prime Minister calls.'

Madoc nodded, satisfied for now.

'And the ravens?'

Randall reached into his jacket pocket. He took out his iPhone. Seven bars lit up, their colours reflected on his face, a mixture of red, amber and green.

'Two dead. Four are sick, although one of them looks close to death,' Randall said, pointing to the reddest of the amber bars. 'Just one bird remains well so far.'

'Good. Not long, then.'

'A few days, sir. Perhaps less.'

'Yes,' Madoc whispered. 'I want to go down to the production floor. There are distribution matters to be finalised for when that idiot politician gives in.'

'Gwendoline's birthday party, sir?'

'Will have to wait. I need to focus on this.'

'She will be...disappointed, Mr Madoc.'

'She won't be when I show her the view from the balcony of Buckingham Palace.'

'Yes, sir.'

The smoked glass door slid open as Madoc approached, then he swept out into the dimly lit corridor beyond, Randall one step behind.

***

Behind the curtains, hiding ready to surprise her father, Gwen's eyes stared wide with horror. She staggered out, her mind reeling.

Dad's responsible for the plague?

And then she remembered the injection she'd had two weeks ago - a new travel jab, he'd told her. Something ready for another exotic holiday he was planning.

I bet it was the vaccine, she thought. So I'm okay. And everybody else can just die for all he cares.

Clammy sweat bubbled across her forehead. She couldn't even begin to take in the madness of it all. She ran from the office with no real plan except to escape into the night.

6

'That was...intense,' said Freddie.

Luca shook his head, trying to clear his thoughts. He felt like he'd been in the world's biggest tumble dryer. Except for a few feathers scattered on the sand, there was no sign that the ravens had ever existed.

'Are you okay?' Jess asked.

'Yeah. I think so. That was all...'

'Like Freddie said, intense.'

Luca looked around, his hands drifting through the soft sand. It stretched away in a gentle arching curve down to a dark lake that looked more like tar than water. The cavern ceiling was too high to be seen, but Luca sensed they were deep underground. A strange glow filled the place, from nowhere and everywhere, a soft cream light like looking at a summer sun through closed eyes. There was a feeling of unimaginable weight, but at the same time it was fresh and light, as if they were sitting at the edge of the sea with the whole world ahead of them. It made no sense after everything that they had been through, but somehow he felt safe.

'We still don't know your name,' Jess said.

'Luca. Wasn't much time for proper introductions back in the lighthouse.'

'We did well there,' said Freddie. 'And the flying was cool. Carried by ravens. Not even sure it's possible, but it happened so it must be. And that lake looks like it might have all kinds of monsters in it, like Loch Ness. That would be cool as well.'

'How old are you, Freddie?' Luca asked.

'Twelve. And four months, if you want me to be accurate.'

'Twelve's fine. You seem a lot older. Aren't you even a little bit scared?'

Freddie paused. For the first time, he looked unsure.

'A bit.'

'I'm scared too. It's okay.'

Jess smiled at that, and her eyes seemed to say thank you for saying the right thing. Luca unexpectedly blushed and looked away.

'So,' he said, keen to change the subject, 'do you want to go first or shall I?'

'I probably don't know much more than you do,' she answered.

'Well, I know absolutely nothing about anything any more, so if you can beat that, I'm all ears.'

How long ago had he been on the school trip? A few hours? Days, even? There was no time line, no sense of normal. Just the insanity of the visions and everything that had happened since.

'I'll tell you what I can,' Jess said, 'then you do the same. Deal?'

'Deal.'

'Our little brother caught the plague first. He's called Josh and he's only two. He likes to sit on my lap and watch Thomas the Tank Engine. Mum and dad got sick and died really quickly. The nurses were really nice but they wouldn't answer any of my questions. A doctor said we had to go to a place with other kids whose parents were dead. I didn't like the sound of that and I argued with him. He said the police were coming. We tried to get away but the ward was locked. Then there was a massive flash of light and the bear was there. The doctor ran away. You would, wouldn't you?'

Luca nodded, transfixed by the way she spoke so calmly. Her eyes never left his.

'The bear turned into a man. He looked friendly enough, but he didn't tell us anything either. Just clicked his fingers and we were by Josh's bed. I touched his hand and he smiled at me. Then we were in the lighthouse. You know the rest.'

'Yeah. Sounds a lot like what happened to me. I was on a school trip. Weird stuff happened. A policeman nearly caught me but the bear scared him off. The man showed me my mum. She's really sick. And then I was with you two. So what the hell does it all mean? And where are we?'

'We don't know.'

'But Jess knows other stuff,' Freddie said. 'Stuff that hasn't even happened yet.'

Jess glared at her brother.

'Not now, Freddie.'

'You just don't want him to think you're weird,' he replied, pouting slightly like a sulky toddler. 'He's going to find out soon enough, when you have another one of your things.'

Luca looked from one to the other, waiting. Neither spoke.

'Stuff that hasn't happened yet?' Luca asked. 'What is that?'

Still silence. Luca crossed his arms.

'If we're going to get along, there can't be any secrets.'

He thought of the photograph in his pocket, and how his mum had known the man, and the girl with red hair, but decided to say nothing for now.

'It's exactly what it sounds like. Jess sees things in her mind. And then they happen. She knew that the man was coming. And she knew about you, days ago.'

Luca's stomach flipped. This was the craziest thing he had heard yet.

'That's impossible,' he said.

'Lots of impossible things have already happened, don't you think?'

Luca went to reply, but Freddie was right. Jess's head was down, her face hidden from him.

'So it's true?' Luca asked.

She nodded.

'Bloody hell. Freddie, can you do it as well?'

'Yes. No. Not yet. I will be able to.'

Luca nodded, although he wasn't so sure that seeing the future was like learning algebra or capital cities.

'So...so, when did it start? You know, the first time?'

'I was three,' Jess replied, her voice barely more than a whisper. 'I told my parents that I'd seen these explosions on underground trains.'

'The London bombs?'

'Yes, a few hours before they happened.'

'It must have freaked them out.'

Jess smiled sadly.

'Not really. They already knew it might happen to one or both of us. My grandmother could do the same. A gift, she called it. Sometimes it feels like a curse when I see bad things. And I can't really control it.'

'She'll get better,' Freddie said. 'Practice makes perfect. If you've got the gift, of course.'

'It's amazing,' Luca said.

'We *are* amazing,' Freddie murmured. 'And maybe you are, too. We'll find out, I suppose.'

I don't feel that amazing, Luca thought. I should have saved mum. I should have got her somewhere safe. I let her down.

'I don't think it would have made any difference at all,' whispered Freddie, his eyes suddenly burning with a strangeness that made Luca shiver.

'Did you just hear what I was thinking?'

'Yeah,' Freddie replied. 'I try not to, but sometimes the thoughts are just too loud.'

He had actually felt Freddie inside his brain like a thin trail of ice.

'Please don't be scared of us,' Jess said. 'Freddie doesn't try to get in people's heads. It's like the thoughts shout at him and he can't ignore them. And sometimes it's only bits of an event that I see, or a name, or a voice. Like a dream when you wake up and it's gone before you can catch the memory.'

'Freddie said you saw me days ago.'

'Your face, that's all. I told Freddie something was going to happen and that we had to be ready. And I was right.'

'Yes,' Freddie added, smiling coldly. 'I know you've got something in your pocket you're not telling us about. No secrets, you said.'

'Fair enough.'

He took out the photograph.

'Me with my dad, the day he flew out to Afghanistan. He was killed. And my mum knew the man.'

He told them what had happened in the flat. There was no point hiding anything.

'What's written on the back?' Jess asked.

Luca turned the photograph over.

'I don't know...I didn't realise there was anything written...' he said, his mouth suddenly dry as the sand under his feet. Jess gently took it from him and read aloud.

'Dear Luca,' she said, 'If you're reading this, I'm dead. Incredible things are going to happen. Be ready. Be smart. Believe, and follow your heart. It will always take you to the right place. I love you so much, my amazing boy. Dad x.'

Luca swallowed hard, his eyes wet with tears.

'Looks like there were plenty of secrets in my family. Things I thought I knew about. And I've been seeing things as well. A red haired kid in a tower. And big birds. Ravens, I guess.'

He stood up and made his way down to the lake.

'Time to find out what else we don't know.' He looked along the curve of the beach, and the rocky walls as they rose up from the sand. 'You two coming?'

'Yeah,' replied Freddie, dusting sand off his jeans. 'Not much point sitting here.'

'We stick together,' Jess agreed, following Luca to the lake. Her fingers brushed against his and a spark of static shot up his arm. 'We look out for each other. Agreed?'

'Agreed.'

7

It was hard going. The sand was so soft their feet almost disappeared with each step, and after a few minutes Luca's legs were aching with the effort, but there wasn't any other choice. They walked for an hour and nothing changed. There was still the lake and the sand, and the harsh rock walls looming over them.

Maybe it never ends, he thought. This is it until we die of thirst.

His lips were dry and he struggled to swallow. He wanted to scoop up a handful of the lake and gulp it down but he didn't think that would be a good idea.

'What's that?' Freddie asked.

'I can't see anything.'

'There. Come on.'

They jogged on about fifty metres, and now Luca saw a series of hexagonal stones rising up out of the sand, one after the other, forming a walkway that led out over the water, each stone just level with the surface as if they were floating.

'Let's see where they go,' he said, and started out along the narrow ribbon.

They edged forwards, three small dark shapes silhouetted against the endless expanse of water that was now all around them. Luca wondered how far they would have to go, and if there was even another side to reach. What if the stones were a trap, designed to slide under if they were trodden on?

Keep going, he told himself, thinking of what his dad had written. Be ready. Be smart.

For a second, he thought he saw tiny lights ahead, but they blinked off when he looked. He slowed and tried to focus on them. Nothing. They walked on, guided by the strange dull glow that seemed to move with them, showing them some of the way but never quite enough.

More lights, pairs of them, flicking on and off.

'Can you see them?'

'Yes,' Jess answered. 'Eyes, aren't they?'

Luca nodded, because he had a feeling they were being watched. After a few minutes, they left the stones and started out across another beach. They were now hemmed in on one side by the rock face and by the lake on the other.

Suddenly, without warning, hundreds of the tiny lights blinked on.

'Careful,' Luca hissed.

'Definitely eyes,' replied Freddie.

Luca smelled them first – the same odour that had filled his nostrils as they were carried from the lighthouse.

'Ravens.'

'Is that good or bad?'

'Don't know.'

The ravens moved out of the shadows and surrounded them, blocking their way back and opening up a narrow path forwards. Their eyes glinted like precious stones, unreal and unsettling. Their massive bodies and lethal beaks were an effective barrier and the children had no choice but to go where they were led along the beach.

Luca tried to step away from the cliff towards the lake but he was immediately pushed back by a raven's wing. The message was clear – go where you're told. The glowing light continued to travel with them, as if they were encased in a vast bowl. Up ahead, Luca saw a dozen black shapes rising out of the gloom. The ravens bundled closer, pushing forwards with excitement. Suddenly, most of them took off in a cloud of warm air and feathers. The rest pushed and pulled the children along.

The shapes were a circle of stone statues, each one an ancient soldier many metres tall. Their swords were drawn ready for battle. The tallest statue wore a small crown and his sword was longer than the others. He held the weapon loosely as if it weighed nothing and his eyes seemed to follow Luca as he edged closer. He shivered, suddenly afraid. The image of the girl at the tower shot through his mind.

'Wow, that was a really loud thought,' Freddie said. 'No way I couldn't hear that. She's strange, isn't she? Like us but different, somehow. And look at that.'

The ravens were swirling up and down in waves, their wings humming and echoing. Dazzling lights flashed out from inside the mass of birds, like a mirror ball spinning at impossible speed. Then a raven shot out and dropped something gold at Freddie's feet. He picked it up and held it out for the others to see - a small gold sword hanging from a chain, a green jewel set in the blade.

A second raven swooped down and landed next to Jess. The bird opened its beak and another sword fell out, this one with a pale blue jewel. She looked at Luca.

'Take it,' he said. 'I think you have to.'

She did, and placed the sword around her neck.

'You okay?'

She nodded, smiling.

'It feels...right. Like it belongs to me. And I can see...oh, I can see things more clearly.'

Jess rubbed her eyes, the smile fading for a moment, but she recovered quickly.

'It's okay. Freddie, put yours on.'

Her brother was already doing just that. The sword nestled snugly against his chest. He looked around him.

'Yeah, I can hear things better. That is very cool.'

A loud squawk next to Luca made him jump. A huge raven waddled towards him and dropped another sword close to his feet. It was gold like the others, with a diamond set into the blade. Luca crouched down and took the sword.

40

All at once, the ravens came down onto them, cackling and flapping with excitement. The children were pushed forwards into the middle of the circle and the statues began to move, each one stretching and changing into real men. They danced and fought against invisible enemies. They screamed silent words. They fell back from unseen blows.

This can't be real, Luca thought. It just can't be.

'What's happening?' he shouted.

'Look!'

One of the statues was kneeling in front of Freddie, his head bowed. Then another did the same to Jess. A prickle of excitement crept up and down Luca's neck, because the tallest statue was approaching him. The statue knelt down and held out his sword so that the tip brushed the top of Luca's head.

A raven flew so close that Luca ducked down, the meaty smell of its breath filling his nostrils. A dark shape lumbered towards them through a curtain of birds, rearing up and solidifying into a snarling bear. The birds' cries were even louder, except now they seemed to be calling in unison, over and over.

'Mer-in! Mer-in!'

The bear threw his enormous paws into the air and roared back. The soldiers turned as one, raising their swords in greeting, their own voices suddenly loud in Luca's head.

'Merlin!'

And then they were statutes again. The ravens flew away into the endless darkness above them, and the bear was gone. Instead, the grey haired man smiled at them. He clicked his fingers and the glowing light erupted into a dazzling display that illuminated the whole cavern. Luca gasped. Rising up out of the sand and carved into the cliff itself, was a vast array of turrets and towers that seemed to stretch on forever.

'Welcome to Camelot,' he said.

8

The Ravenmaster paced anxiously up and down. He stole a glance through the wire mesh of the ravens' sleeping quarters. The remaining birds were huddled together. He breathed in the cold air and listened to the sounds of the city beyond the Tower's walls.

Shouts, screams, a siren, then the unmistakeable crack of gunfire somewhere off to the east. People panicking at the first sign of danger. A city descending into chaos.

'Send in the Army,' he muttered. 'They'll restore order in no time.'

He wandered across the frosty grass of Tower Green. Everything looked the same as it had ever had, quiet and calm. He paused. Three figures were heading his way.

'Oh, great. Just what I need.'

'I'm sorry, sir,' panted a harassed looking Warder. 'He was adamant I let him in.'

'That's fine,' McKenna said. 'Leave this pair with me.'

The Warder headed off, clearly relieved to have escaped so lightly.

'Well, well. And what brings my kid brother and favourite niece out on a night like this?'

'Hello, uncle Sam.'

He looked down, his face softening. The girl smiled from within a thick hooded coat. She held up a dirty stuffed ladybird for him to see.

'Hello, Madeleine. And hello Hug-a-Bug. You both warm enough?'

'Of course we are, silly uncle Sam. Hug-a-Bug doesn't get cold and I'm all wrapped up like an Eskimo.'

'Good girl.'

McKenna's focus shifted to his brother.

'Something important, Jim, or just another excuse to dump Madeleine? She's fourteen, not a baby.' He lowered his voice. 'And I thought you had a carer for her.'

'Yeah, who ran off as soon as the plague started spreading. Emma's got it, if you're remotely interested. She's in hospital and it doesn't look good. I've got to get back to the lab. We're doing all we can to find a vaccine. Is that important enough for you?'

'I'm sorry to hear about Emma,' McKenna sighed.

'Thanks, but that won't help her survive. Helping out with Madeleine for a few days might. I've got work to do.'

The girl was quietly singing nursery rhymes. The Ravenmaster shrugged.

'I don't know. She should be somewhere with other...other kids.'

'Kids like her, you mean?'

'No. yes. Damn it, Jim. I don't know.'

44

'My daughter, Sam. Your niece. She just happens to have Down's syndrome.'

'Emma was the one who always looked for offence in everything I said or did. Now you're doing the same?'

'Not fair.'

'Very fair.'

'Well, that's it, then. Clearly you and I have said all we need to about this.'

'I just never got on with Emma. That was all.'

'You never tried.'

The brothers glared at each other. Madeleine held up her hand.

'Stop fighting,' she said. 'You're both being very naughty.'

Then she returned to her singing.

'She's probably got a point,' said the Ravenmaster.

'So, what's it to be? She either stays here with you or I have to contact the authorities. I'm sure they'll manage to find a foster family.'

'That's not going to happen and you know it. She can stay. Just a few days, though. Then you come and get her. I've got work to do as well.'

'I wouldn't be here unless it was absolutely necessary. And you know how much she's always loved coming to the Tower. It calms her down. Makes her more...manageable.'

'I'm no doctor, Jim.'

'Whatever the reason, it helps. I've brought a bag with some clothes. And some toffees.'

'Her favourites?'

'Of course. I've written down my number at the lab. Straight to my desk. Call me if you need me, okay?'

'You knew I'd say yes. Go on. Get out of here. And Jim...find a way of stopping this thing.'

'We're doing our best, Sam.'

They said their goodbyes. Madeleine gave her dad an enormous hug. She made him kiss Hug-a-Bug before he left. McKenna moved back inside the ravens' quarters, the girl close by his side. She was still singing.

'Ring a ring a roses...ring a ring a roses...ring a ring a roses...'

'Maybe stop that singing, there's a good kid. The ravens might be asleep.'

'Can I see them, uncle Sam? Can I? Can I?'

'They might not want to see you, my darlin'. Some have been a bit poorly.'

'Like mummy,' Madeleine said, squeezing her ladybird even more tightly. 'Oh, look at that one.'

One of the ravens was close to the wire. Its beak worked up and down like a fish trying to breathe out of water, before it flopped forwards into the sawdust. The bird's wings twitched once, then it was over.

And in the Shard, just a mile from where McKenna stood, an amber bar on a tablet screen flicked to red.

9

Gwendoline raced away into the darkness. The snowflakes melted on her skin like iced kisses. She had not expected her escape to be so easy. Surely the doors would be locked. How could she have just walked up the tunnel from the car park and exited the Shard?

Because I did what nobody ever expected me to do, Gwen realised. I left.

Every step took her further from the only world she had ever known. The Shard loomed over her and she paused to look back at it, then she pressed on, head down and eyes half-closed, imagining how angry her father was going to be when he realised she was missing.

'I want him to be more than angry,' she shouted. 'I want him to be scared. And I want him to be sorry.'

Gwen swerved along tunnels and up stone steps. She blundered out onto London Bridge. She had stared down onto it enough times to know where she was. The Thames surged beneath her; the crossing was long and exposed. Snow turned into horrible sleety rain that soaked her hair in seconds. Gwen huddled into her coat as she ran across to the other side. There were only a handful of people around, all wearing the same sucked-in expression of terror.

Gwen hurried off the bridge then turned left and right, going on instinct, trying to avoid eye contact. Cars raced past. Their angry horns jabbed at her ears.

Gwen scurried off into a side-street. Every shop was closed. Shutters were down, padlocks in place. Everywhere she walked, there were dead birds. One shutter had SEE YA NEVER WANNA BE YA sprayed across it. Gwen kept repeating the graffiti motto, the words a steady beat for her running. Any sound was better than the screaming and loud music that seemed to come at her from all sides. She glanced back again. The Shard was like a great glowing lighthouse. Come home, the lights seemed to whisper. Turn around and return. He won't even know you've been away. You can slot back in safe and sound as his virus kills.

Gwen kept going, head down, not wanting to give up so easily. The minutes merged together into hours. The streets were quieter now. She realised she had not seen anybody for a while. The horns were muffled, the sounds of the city carried away from her by a harsh wind that swept down the buildings.

Gwen tried to remember some of the street names she had seen, hoping to be able to trace her way back if she needed to – Fenchurch Street, Aldgate, onto Whitechapel Road. A car slowed down. The driver leaned out. His eyes were bloodshot and there were bruises on his face.

'Run away before it's too late!'

He laughed insanely, his car flicking from side to side, nearly bumping into another coming in the opposite direction. Gwen doubled back on herself to get away. She was soon tangled in a mass of narrow alleys and boxy flats. Throbbing beats pounded out from one. Somewhere, a woman howled. She heard raucous laughter, a baby crying. At the corner of Langdale Street and Ponler Street, she jumped away as a massive dog growled and slobbered at her. Wet bloody feathers were stuck to its jaws. Gwen ran, the tears prickling her eyes.

I'm so lost, she thought. I should have stayed at home.

Home. The word felt like a bad joke.

The Shard was still there, but the pale yellow glow of the upper floors now looked more like a sneer than a friendly smile.

Gwen didn't hear the men approach until one of them coughed wetly. She spun around. They were obviously unwell. Their faces were pale and they shivered uncontrollably. The coughing man spat out a thick blood-stained glob onto the slushy pavement.

'You need help, little girl?'

Gwen didn't answer. Her tongue was glued to the top of her mouth. She flicked her eyes left and right, looking for a way to run.

'Don't be scared,' the coughing man's friend whispered.

He scratched at his neck with a bruised hand.

49

'We won't hurt you. Will we, Robbie?'

His mate was too busy hacking up more blood to care.

'No, we won't,' non-cougher continued. 'Just give us whatever money you've got. And that tasty looking watch.'

He cocked his head to one side, eyes narrowed.

'Not caught the plague yet? Don't worry. You soon will.'

He started to laugh, a high-pitched hysterical sound that made Gwen's teeth tingle. She moved away. And then she jumped and screamed. Somebody had grabbed her by the shoulders.

***

'Run,' a voice said.

Gwen froze. Her brain yelled at her legs to move but every connection was scrambled, every muscle paralysed.

'Then I'll carry you.'

Gwen was dragged backwards away from the sickly men. She could not breathe. She could not fight back.

'Help me a bit here, eh?'

'What?'

The grip on her shoulders relaxed a little.

'Oh, good. I was starting to think you didn't speak English.'

The men were fifty metres away now. The bruised one collapsed next to his friend. The risk of attack was gone.

'They don't look so scary from here.'

It was a boy's voice. He started to laugh. That was enough to snap her back to her senses. She kicked out and felt her shoe heel connect with bone. It made a satisfying crunch and she was suddenly free. She span around with her fists up. The boy was no older than her. He was down on the ground, hugging his shin.

'What did you do that for? I was trying to save you.'

He wasn't crying but looked as if he might at any moment. The boy bit down on his lip, his eyes flashing. In spite of everything Gwen smiled. He looked like his pride was as badly hurt as his leg.

'Sorry,' said Gwen. 'I thought you were kidnapping me. I was just protecting myself.'

'I'm not a kidnapper,' the boy groaned. 'And don't think you had me beaten. Just a lucky kick, that's all.'

He glared as he tested his leg on the ground. Gwen was relieved to see there didn't seem to be much wrong.

'Looks okay,' she said.

'How do you know? It's not *your* leg that nearly got broken. Still can't believe you did it.'

'Well, I did. I've said sorry. There isn't much more I can do, is there?'

That didn't seem to help. The boy turned away, hobbling.

'Find your own way home, rich girl.'

'You're going to just leave me here? How dare you! Do you have any idea who I am?'

51

She regretted the words as soon as they came out. This wasn't the time or the place to be advertising her identity. The boy stopped.

'No. Give me a clue.'

'Forget it. It's not important.' She decided to start again. 'Look, are you sure you're all right?'

The boy stamped his injured leg a few more times.

'Sorted. Just a scratch.'

He grinned and Gwen saw he had a handsome open face when he wasn't scowling. She smiled back. At that moment he was the closest thing to a friend she had.

'I'm pleased. I wouldn't want to think of you losing a fight with a girl.'

'Wouldn't be the first time,' he said. 'You don't know the girls round here. And what were you doing talking to strangers in a friendly bit of town like this?'

'I took a wrong turn, that's all. I know the way home.'

'Yeah?'

'Yes, I do.'

Gwen glanced up at the Shard. The boy did the same.

'That's home? You're even richer than I thought.'

'I'm not that rich,' Gwen said, not sure what else to say.

He wasn't fooled and they both knew it. He pointed at her watch. 'That came out of a Christmas cracker, did it?'

'Very funny,' she replied with more sarcasm than she meant. 'Sorry.'

'You've said sorry twice already. And if you want to leave, feel free. I won't stop you.'

They stood facing each other for a few moments. Neither spoke. The boy grinned again. His eyes sparkled.

'You haven't got a clue where you are, have you? Well, princess, today's your lucky day. You'll be okay if you stick with me.'

Gwen looked more closely at him. He was taller than her, slim and athletic under the baggy clothes. His skin was smooth, his eyes deepest brown above high cheekbones. The grin made him look younger than he was but she could tell the boy was street-wise and tough, attributes she didn't have. There was a tension about him, as though he was ready for something to happen.

'I'm not your princess, thank you very much.'

He held her gaze, then his head flicked to one side.

'Whatever. I can hear more people coming. Time to be somewhere else.'

He turned and headed off. Gwen didn't follow.

'Where are you going?'

'Away from here. Come with me, if you like. I'll look after you. Or you could stay right where you are.'

He disappeared into the shadows, then reappeared an instant later. Gwen saw a glimmer of gold around his neck that she hadn't seen before. He drew closer. It was a small sword on a chain. A stone flashed from the cross-piece, blood-red and dazzlingly beautiful.

'Oh, I'm Carter,' the boy muttered, shoving the sword out of sight. Then he was gone again before Gwen had a chance to speak. Gwen only hesitated long enough to hear the sound of approaching feet and shouting. Then she did the only thing that seemed to make any sense. She followed the boy into the darkness.

10

Madoc took a small bite from a biscuit. His back was to the window. He didn't need to look out onto the city to know what was happening down there. How could he not know? He recalled the test subject - a homeless drifter, enticed with a promise of food and a bed for the night. Instead, he got to share a cell with an infected bird.

First there was a terrible fever. Then lots of coughing, wet and painful. Burst blood vessels in the eyes and gums, with bruises all over the skin. Breathlessness soon followed, with rising panic as liquid flooded into the lungs. The lucky ones would die in a few hours of that stage developing. The unlucky ones might struggle on for another day or two.

The vans that carried the deadly cargo had driven to the Essex marshes in the depths of the night, their drivers breathing carefully behind masks. They had released a thousand sick pigeons.

Madoc put the biscuit down.

I had no choice, Madoc told himself. What's a few million dead in the grand scheme of things? Many more will die because of war and hunger. And when I'm in control everything will be different.

Randall entered the office, his face serious.

'Randall, what is it?' Madoc asked.

Randall seemed hesitant. That was unlike him. He was usually calm and controlled.

'What is it, Randall?' Madoc repeated.

'Sir, it's Gwendoline.'

'What about her?'

'She's left the Shard.'

'Say that again, Randall,' he whispered. 'Say it very slowly.'

'She's gone, sir. Just walked out. I've got teams on the ground searching for her.'

'Tell me this isn't happening.'

'I understand your concern, but the plague can't harm her. The vaccine is 100% effective.'

'I know that, Randall. It cost me two hundred million pounds to develop, if you remember.'

'Yes, sir. Of course.'

'My daughter is missing in a city that's going to descend into total anarchy in the next few days. Which bit of that shouldn't concern me?'

Madoc's mobile phone buzzed. He scrambled for it and stared at the screen. The colour drained from his face.

'It's from her.'

He turned the phone round for Randall to see.

'I know what you've done,' Randall read out.

'Get her back,' Madoc whispered. 'Now.'

'My men will find her, sir. I promise you that.' Randall's gaze dropped before he spoke again. 'Her birthday - what a day for her to find out what we've done.'

'You're lucky I don't have you thrown from the top of this building.'

Randall didn't reply.

'You know when to shut up, I'll give you that. Now get out of my sight.'

Randall left without another word. Madoc stood in terrible silence, his eyes closed, his hands clenched. Gwendoline's text ran through his head again and again.

I know what you've done..I know...I know...

11

'Need to go west,' Carter said, hurrying Gwen along.

Gwen stared at the screen of her iPhone for a few seconds. There was no reply from her father. She threw the phone away, wincing slightly as it smashed into a wall.

'Keep walking,' Carter urged again, pulling at her wrist. His fingers snagged under the bracelet of her watch. Gwen tugged herself free.

'I'm tired, Carter. I'm not going any further until you tell me where we're going.'

'You all right?' a passing woman asked, waving a large knife. 'Need some help with your boyfriend?'

Carter pulled open his jacket to reveal a gun in a holster. The woman backed away.

'Fair enough, kid. You play it your way.'

The woman wandered off into the maze of streets. They were alone again.

'Where did you get that gun?' Gwen asked.

'Doesn't matter where,' he replied. 'Just be glad I did. We need to get out of the city. This place is full of sick people. Have you forgotten already?'

Gwen shuddered.

'Of course not.'

'Good. This is a mean place when it wants to be.'

'I can't go anywhere. I can't go home,' Gwen whispered.

Her voice cracked and she slumped down onto the pavement.

'No? Well, that makes two of us. I haven't got a home to go to either.'

Gwen looked at Carter more closely. He was strange, unlike anybody she had ever met before. There was a cocky sureness about him but she sensed he needed to be liked.

'I ran away,' she said.

'Plenty do. Why did you?'

'Something...something about my dad.'

Carter sat down next to her. He handed her a bottle of water. Gwen drank deeply then used the rest to wash her face. The empty bottle rattled away across the street.

'Sorry,' Gwen said. 'I used it all up.'

'Don't supposed you're used to sharing.'

Gwen looked down, her cheeks colouring.

'I'm only joking,' he said. 'We can get more. Anyway, you were saying something about your dad. I never knew mine. He died when I was a baby.'

Gwen nodded, unsure what else to do or say.

'Mum got sick,' Carter continued. 'So did my brother. He's older than me, and bigger. A proper bad boy. He kicked me out - told me to get away. I know he did it to protect me but it was still hard, leaving them like that. I've just been wandering around, keeping safe and out of trouble. Then something made me go down that street. It was like I knew you were going to be there.'

Carter paused.

'What's your name, anyway?'

'Gwendoline. Or Gwen, if you like.'

He did a mock bow, swinging an arm across his chest.

'I'm very pleased to meet you, Gwen.'

She smiled at that.

'Likewise. What's your first name?'

'Carter's just fine.'

There was a moment's silence between them, broken only by the sounds of the city unravelling around them.

'So,' Carter continued, 'you running away from your dad?'

'I don't really want to talk about it.'

'Fair enough. Let me know when you do. I'm a good listener. Are you coming with me, then? It's a long way to where I'm going.'

'Where is it?'

'Somewhere west,' Carter said. 'Devon, I think. I don't know exactly. I suppose I'll know when I get there. It might sound mad but I just know I've got to go and find some other kids. I...I dreamed about them.'

He looked embarrassed, and suddenly not so cocky.

'I've never been outside of London. And I bet you think I'm some kind of lunatic. Don't blame you. I thought that myself when it happened, but the dream was so real. I just have to go. And there's nothing left here for me now.'

Gwen clambered to her feet. Should she trust him? At that moment, she wasn't sure she had much of a choice. She took a deep breath.

'That chunk of gold around your neck - why don't you tell me all about it?'

Carter lifted out the sword.

'I didn't nick it,' he said defensively. 'I found it. I was down by a canal, under a bridge. It was cold and I was out of the wind, but that wasn't why I was there. I don't actually know why, it just felt right. Then the weirdest thing happened. This massive bird landed next to me. It was like a crow, but bigger. I was a bit scared, you know? I reckon it could have taken my eyes out if it wanted.'

'Bigger than a crow? It was probably a raven.'

'A raven,' repeated Carter, rolling the word around his mouth like he was tasting it. 'Maybe. Anyway, I sat there just looking at it. Then the bird did something crazy and this is the honest truth, I swear.'

'Go on. I'll believe you.'

'Okay' he said. 'That bird opened its mouth and the sword just fell out, right on the floor.'
Gwen stared at him.

'This is for real? This actually happened?'

He looked hurt. 'You said you'd believe me.'

'I do. I think I've read about that kind of things. Crows and magpies and ravens, they like bright shiny things. And sometimes they'll bring them to people.'

'What? A raven gave me a present?'

'Yes. It looks like it's worth a fortune, and I should know.'

'Don't care what it's worth,' he said. 'It just makes me feel stronger when I'm wearing it.'

Carter moved closer. His eyes danced with excitement.

'And I think it's something to do with the dream. I need to go west, to an island. There's more swords there like this one. Come with me. You'll see.'

Gwen hesitated. She wondered if he was sick with the plague. Maybe the first stage was madness.

'You think I'm making it all up,' he said.

'I'd be crazy not to.'

'Then we're both crazy, because it happened just like I said. And I'm going whatever you believe so make your mind up. Stay here or come with me.'

How much should she tell this boy? And what if he really was infected? Gwen weighed up her options. He seemed friendly enough, and the sword intrigued her. She decided to stay with him, for now.

'Listen,' she said, 'this is really important. You might be in danger with me tagging along. My dad will come looking for me and he's not the kind of person you want to annoy.'

'Don't worry,' said Carter, letting her see the gun once more. 'I can look after myself. And you if I have to, although your fancy karate kicks might come in handy.'

'Thanks,' Gwen replied, 'but you won't be able to look after either of us when he finds me. Trust me on that one.'

'Why? What makes you so special?'

The question was simple enough. A truthful answer would change everything. Gwen took a deep breath.

'My dad's John Madoc. You've probably heard of him.'

'The guy who owns the news?'

Gwen frowned. That just about summed up her father.

'Yeah.'

'Multi-millionaire John Madoc? Homes all over the world? Yachts and private jets and all that stuff?'

'Okay. Don't push it.'

'Madoc's kid out here in the big bad city. Interesting.' Carter scratched his chin. 'What have you done that's so bad? Been cruel to your polo ponies?'

'I can't tell you any more at the moment,' Gwen said. 'You've got to trust me.'

'I don't trust anybody with anything. That's how I get by.'

Gwen's eyes flashed with anger.

'Suit yourself,' she snarled. 'I can look after myself if I have to.'

'Really? Feel free.'

Gwen crossed her arms, defeated. Out here, with no money or phone, she was about as safe as a mouse on a motorway.

'I don't like the way you spoke to me.'

'My big mouth got me expelled from Eton.'

'Very funny.'

Gunfire rattled somewhere close, followed by screams and the smashing of glass. Gwen jumped closer to Carter. He wrapped her up in his arms and they danced awkwardly for a moment, neither knowing what to do. Gwen pulled away and she started to cry. There was no way to stop the tears.

'I'm sorry,' she said. 'I'm just so scared.'

The sobs racked her body as he held her.

'Don't worry,' Carter murmured, his face close to hers. 'I'm scared every day on the streets. It's how I stay alive. Are you sure you can't go home? Maybe that would be the best thing to do.'

Gwen glanced up at the Shard. Carter followed her stare.

'No,' she said. 'Too late for that.'

'Decision made, then. You're coming with me.'

Gwen nodded.

'First you've got to tell me where you got the gun. Did you hurt anybody?'

Carter frowned.

'I'm not a killer, if that's what you mean. I found it on a dead body. Let's hope we don't have to use it, eh?'

'Let's hope so.'

The sounds of the city faded for a moment, and Gwen heard soft footsteps.

'Move away from him, miss. We'll take over from here.'

12

The gold sword hung around Luca's neck like a convict's chain. He wanted to rip it off and hurl it at the man. Fear, anger, disbelief, excitement...the emotions swept through him in an unstoppable wave.

'Who the hell are you?' he croaked.

'Steady,' the man said. 'You'll have lots of questions.'

'You're damn right about that.'

'Try and stay calm. We can talk it all through.'

'My mum said I shouldn't talk to strangers,' Luca said, trying to sound older and braver than he felt. 'She's the one you left behind, remember?'

'Of course. And I know you're Luca, Jess and Freddie. My name's Peake.'

The man moved in a little closer. Luca could smell him, a mixture of wood smoke, earth and wet fur like a dog that's been in the rain.

'Now we're not strangers any more.'

Peake held out a meaty hand to shake. Luca stared down at it, expecting to see hairs sprout across the lined skin. A faded tattoo of a bear was just visible. Luca didn't take the hand. The man shrugged and pulled it away.

'I could have saved her,' Luca shouted. 'You left her lying there!'

'No. She's too sick with the plague.'

'She knew you.'

'Yes. She knows my name. I've had lots of them down the years. I die, I change, I come back with a new one.'

The man was still smiling, standing there in his coat and jeans as if he was waiting for a bus, except people at bus stops don't normally talk about how many times they've died.

'Die? Change? And this place...that lighthouse...what is all this?'

The questions tumbled out of Luca.

'Slow down. I know it's all a lot to take in, but it'll make sense. I promise.'

'She knew you,' Luca repeated.

Peake nodded.

'And these statues came to life. I can turn into a bear. There are thousands of ravens in here and you're looking at an impossible underground castle. Crazy, eh?'

'Tell me how you do the bear thing,' said Freddie.

'Where to begin?'

'Just tell me.'

Peake raised an eyebrow.

'Say please.'

'No,' the boy replied, and Peake laughed out loud.

'Simple, Freddie. I used magic. That police officer and the doctor saw me but I think they'll forget soon enough. Maybe it's all a bit of undigested beef or a crumb of cheese, they might say.'

'Scrooge said that,' Freddie said.

'You know your Dickens. Clever boy. Just don't try to be too clever, eh? And I did the same with the lighthouse full of snow. That was a test, by the way, and I'm very pleased you all came through without getting hurt.'

'Hang on,' Luca said, anger stirring in him again, 'It was a test? Bloody hell, we were nearly killed in there!'

'You weren't and that's all that mattered. This place doesn't let just anybody in, by the way. You've got to be...' Peake paused. 'What word would you use, Freddie?'

'Special.'

'That's right. You are. And that lighthouse is now back to normal, up on the surface. And there's no magical storm raging, or great clouds of ravens. Life goes on. Nobody knows you're here.'

'What?' Luca said, fists balled. 'That all sounds like a threat.'

'No, son. Just fact. You're not here because of me. You're here because of you. Like your friend said, you're special.'

'I saw you in my head, before you came to the hospital. I knew you were coming.'

Peake looked at Jess.

'Gift of sight, eh? Well, that could be a big help. And you, Freddie. You're staring at me like you're trying to burrow into my brain. That's good as well. All these skills and talents. Gives you a better chance of success.'

'I can't get in, though,' said Freddie. 'Maybe because you don't want me to.'

'Maybe you're right.'

'Success at what?' interrupted Luca. 'You're not telling us anything.' He held up the gold sword. 'Like what these are.'

'The ravens have been busy. I imagine you were given that by my friend, here.'

Peake glanced at the biggest raven, hopping and chattering nearby.

'That's Bran. The Latin name for the common raven is *Corvus corax,* except there's nothing very common about him.'

The raven was easily half a metre high with a beak that was nearly as long as Luca's hand. Without warning, he stretched out his wings and flapped them twice. Luca ducked and fell back.

'Steady, Bran,' laughed Peake. 'Don't scare our guests.'

'Crazy bird,' Luca muttered, surprised and embarrassed at the same time. 'He'd better not try that again.'

'I'm afraid Bran does pretty much whatever he wants, son. Bet you're a bit like that, eh?'

Luca didn't reply.

'Thought so.'

'You said this was Camelot,' Freddie said. 'So that means King Arthur and his knights. That's who the statues are.'

'Well done. Have a prize.'

Peake flipped a chocolate bar at Freddie, from a hand that had been empty a moment before.

'Magic, but still tasty.'

King Arthur...Luca stared up at the motionless stone warrior who had touched him, trying to make any sense of what he was hearing.

'The statues called you Merlin,' he said.

'They did.'

'Like the wizard in the Arthur stories?'

'The very same, but I haven't actually been called Merlin for two thousand years. And they're not stories.'

Luca glanced at the others. Jess was pale but calm. Freddie was leaning forward like a begging dog.

'Say that again,' Luca said. 'Two thousand years?'

'You heard. And I know you can't believe it, but it's true. Look around you. Think of everything you've seen. The impossible is very much possible.'

Peake waved his hands across his face. He changed into the bear then back to a man.

'Magic's everywhere, if you look hard enough.'

Peake waved his hands again. His face flattened and stretched into a younger man with long brown hair. Another wave changed him into a boy no older than Freddie. Then Luca saw an eagle, then a rat. More animals followed - fox, badger, mole and dog. Finally Peake's face returned to normal.

'You want to know about me? I started my life screaming in a cave with nothing but wet slate for a bed. My mother didn't survive my birth and my father was eaten by starving wolves. I was found by a wandering shepherd and raised as his son. His wife taught me the magic of her ancestors and gave me the name Merlin.'

'They died when I was about your age, Luca. I drifted from place to place. Somehow, I came to this island, near to where the lighthouse now stands. I found lots of ravens waiting for me. I found Bran. Time moved on, and Arthur became king of the Britons.'

Bran flapped his wings and moved in close to Luca, leaning against him, claws flexing against his shin.

'Bran's older than me and twice as wise. He likes you. That's a big deal, son.'

Luca touched Bran's head, unsure and nervous of what the bird might do. The feathers were warm and slightly greasy. He could feel the power in Bran's muscles. His fingers tingled, as if something magical was passing into him.

'He'll look after you if you let him,' Peake said. 'And the other birds will do whatever Bran says.'

Peake stretched. The joints in his shoulders cracked and he grimaced with pain.

'So, let me tell you about Arthur. Then you'll understand why you're here.'

13

Carter was staring over Gwen's shoulder. He looked like a cornered animal, all bunched up and ready to spring. His fingers twitched towards his jacket where the gun was hidden.

'Keep your hands out, sonny, or I'll shoot you before you even know I've done so.'

Gwen turned. Two men were approaching. They wore dark combat clothes, their heads covered by balaclavas. Their rubber-soled boots made virtually no sound and their machine guns were pointed directly at Carter.

'My father's men,' Gwen whispered. 'Don't do anything stupid.'

'Don't plan to,' Carter replied. He sounded calmer than he should.

'She's coming with us, kid,' one of the men growled. 'Give her back whatever you've stolen, then turn around and kneel down.'

Gwen's heart slammed in her chest. This was only going to end one way.

'He hasn't robbed me,' she pleaded. 'He helped me.'

The weapons wavered for the briefest of seconds, but the moment soon passed.

'Sorry, miss. We have our orders. Anybody who has interacted with you is to be...removed from the situation.'

'Killed, you mean. You're going to murder him.'

'Don't make this difficult, miss. You're coming back to the Shard if I have to carry you all the way there myself.'

The man reached for Gwen's wrist and pulled her close.

'Do it,' he shouted. 'Then we're out of here.'

His colleague nodded. Carter stared defiantly at him, his eyes burning with hatred.

'Go on, just like your brave friend says.'

'My pleasure,' muttered the man, taking aim. He never had the chance to fire. He groaned and fell forwards, a kitchen knife buried in his neck.

'Get the other one,' a female voice screamed.

Knife woman was back and this time she wasn't alone. A dozen other people tumbled out of the shadows. Gwen fell away from the man's grasp as he was attacked. His machine gun spluttered, shooting down four of the mob, but then the gun jammed and the man collapsed under the fury of the attack. Gwen caught a final glimpse of his eyes. He knew he was going to die as he disappeared beneath a hail of blows.

When it was over, the woman removed her blade with a horrible wet sucking sound. She wiped it on the dead man's clothes and turned to face Gwen.

'We saw these two coppers heading your way,' she said. 'They killed my friend for nothing a few streets away. I reckon you were next. Well, they won't kill anybody else, will they?'

73

Gwen shook her head, grateful that the woman had mistaken the men for police. She didn't plan to correct her on who they actually were.

'Get out of here,' the woman said. 'We're on your side. The next lot might not be.'

'Thanks,' Carter said. He grabbed Gwen's hand. 'Time to be somewhere else.'

The woman moved in close, out of earshot of the others. She prodded a grubby finger against Carter's chest and fixed him with a cold stare.

'You and miss Madoc need to stick together. Look after her.'

Then she turned and ran.

'How do you know me?' Gwen shouted.

'Let's worry about that later, yeah?' Carter said, tugging at her.

They ran as well, heading west.

14

'Arthur was the son of King Uther Pendragon,' Peake began. They were sat in the circle of statues, surrounded by ravens. Bran had settled down next to Luca, like a faithful Labrador after a long walk. Peake had provided them with food and drink just by waving his hands. Luca didn't know if any of it was real. He was too hungry to care. 'He became king himself when he was fourteen.'

'Same age as me,' Luca said, holding out a chicken wing. Bran gulped it down in one and Luca grinned. He was starting to like it here.

'Big responsibility. There aren't many who could handle it at that age. His best friend was a knight called Mordred. They were closer than brothers. A year after Arthur took the crown, a massive earthquake struck. Whole towns were destroyed. Arthur rescued Mordred by rolling a huge rock off him. He did it with the natural magic that was in him.'

Magic, thought Luca. Such a stupid little word. Up until the moment Peake had appeared out of nowhere he would have laughed at anybody claiming there was such a thing. Not any more.

'Arthur was a brilliant leader. He brought all the tribes together under one flag and ruled with wisdom beyond his years. This place was the centre of everything.'

Peake took off his coat and shirt to reveal four tattoos - a bear on one arm, a dragon on the other. A great eagle flew across his back. Over his heart, an Irish wolf snarled.

'To begin with, Mordred was Arthur's most loyal knight, but he had a dark secret. He believed his own family should rule. He became twisted by jealousy. He changed his name to Madoc, the name of his ancestors.'

'Madoc...like the media guy?' Luca asked.

Peake's eyes narrowed.

'Yes, of course. The Madocs have always been full of hate. I'll show you.'

Peake waved his arms. A pale shape formed in the air. Bran tensed. Luca saw the thin figure of a man carrying a blood-stained sword.

'Watch.'

The beach and lake faded away. They were in a frozen forest. Mist clung to the skeleton branches of stunted trees. The cries of wild animals echoed around them.

'This is what happened back then.'

The man stumbled past. His eyes were wild and staring.

'That's Madoc. He tried to steal the crown but he failed. He killed some of Arthur's men and escaped.'

Peake waved again. They were now in a dark stinking cave. Fetid water dripped into green pools. Rats scurried around their feet, and Luca had to tell himself over and over it wasn't real, such was the terror he felt. Madoc sat in the shadows, thin and gaunt, his beard long, his clothes no more than filthy rags. He was muttering to himself, a rapid stream of nonsense and gibberish. Every few moments, he grabbed at a pile of old bones and threw them down, studying the shapes they made.

'Learning the darkest magic that exists,' Peake said. 'The ravens reported back to me what he was doing. I tried to warn Arthur but he was too proud and arrogant to believe there was any danger.'

Another ghostly figure drifted into view. He wore a long cloak and a simple headband of white bark.

'That's me, all those years ago. I found Madoc. I begged him to stop but it was too late. The magic had driven him insane. He attacked me without warning. I was lucky to get away. I had to rest for weeks, to let the wounds heal. By then Madoc was heading back to Camelot, full of anger and hate and ready for war.'

A new terrifying scene formed. Thousands of wild men surged towards them, each armed with swords and axes, their bodies painted with strange blue shapes. They wore necklaces of bone. Some carried skulls on sticks.

'Madoc gathered an army. All they wanted was to fight and kill. He gave them that chance.'

Luca shivered as the warriors swarmed down through the mist.

'I couldn't hold them back. They reached the island. Camelot was at their mercy.'

Peake's voice broke with the trauma of it. His eyes filled with tears and the scene changed again. They were surrounded by hundreds of crying children, their faces pinched with hunger and fear.

'Arthur led his knights out to face the enemy. A bitter wind whipped up the waves and the sandstorm cut their skin like a million tiny knives. Arthur raised his standard. The horns blared and the battle began.'

It appeared just as it had been. Luca recoiled from the cold and the bloodshed even though he knew it wasn't real. Swords swung against armour. Screams filled the air. Thousands of ravens flew amongst the battling armies. Bodies lay ten deep.

'It was brutal,' Peake shouted above the din. 'War always is.'

The knights were being forced back. Rain hammered onto mud-spattered men fighting for their lives. Each time one of Madoc's warriors was cut down, another ten seemed to fill the gap in the lines. The knights regrouped in a loose horseshoe, swords pointing outwards.

'I would have fought bravely,' said Freddie in a dull voice.

'I think you're right,' said Peake.

Luca winced at the sounds of weapons clashing, of men dying. He stared at Peake.

'Where were you? Couldn't you do anything to help?'

He hadn't meant to accuse the man, but Peake closed his eyes and hung his head.

'I'm sorry, Luca. I was too weak. My magic was no use. I can remember every horrible moment as if it's happening now. The shame never goes away.'

The scene changed to the cavern, just as they were now. The battle continued to rage around them. Madoc's men were forcing the last few knights across the lake. The tall figure of King Arthur swung his great sword left and right. Blood dripped from his hands. His face was a mask of anger and despair. Luca recognised him as the statue that had bowed before him.

'I want to go and help!' he screamed. 'We could do it!'

'You can't change history. What you're seeing is done.'

Yet again, everything changed. Luca saw Madoc in his black armour, a glittering diamond skull across his shield. Arthur's head was bare. His wounds dripped blood into the lake.

'King Arthur's last stand,' Peake shouted as the king launched himself at his treacherous friend.

Their swords smashed against each other. It was clear that Madoc was stronger but Arthur was not going to give in. Even as he collapsed down onto the stones he tried to inflict a killer blow but Madoc jumped out of the way. He slashed Arthur's hands and face.

'I'm the real Pendragon!'

Then he plunged his sword down for a final time. It passed through Arthur into the causeway and the king was engulfed in unnatural green flames. His body burned away until there was nothing left but flakes of black soot floating in the air.

'My anger exploded like never before,' Peake said. 'I used my magic to destroy. I turned Madoc and his army into beetles. The ravens swooped down and ate them all. Those beautiful birds didn't stop until every single insect was gone.'

Peake was quiet for a moment. The ghostly shapes faded away.

'The surviving knights headed for the mainland. There was nothing left for them here.'

A sad procession of wounded men and their families trudged past, heads bowed, wounds bandaged. Each knight wore a small gold sword around his neck.

'I made them from the shattered remnants of Arthur's sword. Whatever magic I could still create was poured into them, so that if a Madoc ever threatened Britain again, they could come together against him. And King Arthur faded from history and became a myth.'

Suddenly, Bran threw back his head and screeched like a knife across a blackboard. All the other birds joined him in a deafening cacophony.

'We'll have company soon,' Peake said. 'The ravens can sense more of you out there.'

'Coming here?' asked Luca. 'Who? When?'

'I don't know. I can't keep track of all the swords. You three have been hard enough to find.'

'I think I've seen them,' Jess said, her eyes closed. 'They're escaping danger, trying to get here.'

'When was this?' Peake asked.

'In the lighthouse, before Luca arrived. My head was full of all sorts of things. I didn't know what it meant but now I understand.'

'They'll have their own tests to overcome,' Peake added, 'to be worthy.'

'So they might die trying,' Luca groaned. 'You could go and bring them.'

'No, son. It doesn't work that way. I'm not a God. I can only do so much, then the magic is gone for a while. Look at me closely. See how much I've aged already just from all I've done today.'

It was true. Peake's hair was greyer, balding in patches. There were new lines around his eyes and he seemed too small for his clothes.

'You're like the Ghost of Christmas Present,' laughed Freddie, swallowing down the last cube of chocolate.

'You really do know your Dickens,' Peake replied.

'But what are we here for?'

'The plague, son. Have you wondered where it's come from? It's dark magic and it's killing the ravens at the Tower of London.'

'So?'

'So if the ravens die, Britain falls. Simple as that. You lot have got to stop it happening.'

They all started speaking at once, a babble of voices that echoed around the cavern. Peake held up a hand.

'Enough. I can't tell you any more because that's all I know. Like I said, I'm not a God.'

'Is that it?' Luca asked. 'You've told us nothing!'

'Telling is never as good as showing, son. Use your eyes. Look at what's in front of you. All the real magic is in there. When the others arrive go into Camelot and find Arthur's hall. Bran will show you the way and the swords will do the rest. I have to go now, but I'll be back soon. Then we can talk some more.'

And with a click of his fingers, he vanished.

15

'Killed by a mob, Randall,' Madoc said as they watched the playback from the dead men's head-cams. The footage told its own story.

'What happened to their training? What am I paying for?'

'They came from nowhere, sir,' Randall replied. 'It was impossible to stop the attack.'

'Impossible? A word for weaklings. You're losing your touch.'

Madoc punched a fist against his thigh. Something niggled him, something he had seen on the playback.

'Play the film again.'

The grainy images flickered across the screen. Madoc leaned in closer, concentrating.

'Stop!' he shouted. 'There! Look at that, Randall. Look at that!'

Randall did not move. A muscle under one eye twitched. His lips were tight.

'Tell me I'm right!'

'Yes, sir. I should have seen that.'

The image from the head-cam showed Gwen illuminated by the harsh street lights, her eyes wide with fear. A boy's arms were wrapped around her. His face was blurred but the camera had captured a flash of something gold and dark red, like a drop of blood.

'It's one of the swords,' Madoc said.

'Yes, sir.'

'What does this mean, Randall?'

Randall hesitated, and Madoc turned like a starving lion.

'Answer me! What does this mean?'

Randall's reply was measured and calm.

'Gwendoline appears to be with a youth who is in possession of one of the twelve swords of Camelot, sir. I cannot explain how or indeed why.'

'And you missed this?'

'I did. I apologise.'

'Damn you, Randall! I've spent my entire life looking for them and now one shows up around the neck of a city rat who's with my daughter!'

Randall was silent. His eyes gave nothing away. Madoc's anger was like a hurricane sucking everything into it.

'This is no coincidence, Randall. This is Merlin. He's definitely gathering them all together.'

'We have to assume that, sir.'

'And Gwen's still alive. I know she is.'

'Yes, sir. The boy seems to be looking after her.'

'Gwen's phone?'

'We've hacked into the signal. It's dead. No calls out and no more texts.'

'There's another way to track her movements. Use the GPS built into her watch.'

'I'll send fifty men immediately,' Randall said.

Madoc smiled.

'Perhaps Gwendoline's stupidity will bring about a happy ending for us all.'

***

The stolen motorbike was great for manoeuvring through the jams of abandoned cars but its tank was nearly dry. A sign said there was a service station in a mile.

They bounced over the rutted road, skidding on ice patches. Gwen was getting used to Carter's crazy driving but it didn't make it any less scary when he opened up the throttle. In spite of the cold, Gwen was sweating under the helmet and leather jacket. She tried not to think about the owner of the bike shop back in London. Carter had waved his pistol at him but there was no need. The man was already half dead.

The journey had been horribly chaotic. Gangs roamed the streets, people were barricaded into their homes. They heard plenty of gunfire and saw dead bodies more than once. There weren't many police around.

'A uniform won't stop the plague,' Carter said as they picked their way west.

The ones who were supposed to be in charge were hiding just the same as everybody else. Every mile increased the distance between Gwen and her old life, and every mile hardened her heart a fraction more. It was just her and Carter now.

And his dream, she reminded herself. He believes in it so much. And if he believes, then so do I.

The woman with the knife had known her. How was that possible? What was happening? Too many questions and not enough answers. She was dizzy with the madness of it all.

Carter turned off the road and coasted up to service station. He pushed up his visor and Gwen did the same.

'Fill up, check if there's any food left, then we go. No more than five minutes, yeah?'

Gwen nodded. Carter climbed off and tried the pump. Petrol splashed onto the tarmac.

'Bingo,' he said.

The whole place seemed deserted except for a solitary magpie in a nearby tree.

'Over there,' said Gwen.

'Seen it,' Carter replied. 'Looks healthy enough. Not caught your dad's cold yet, eh?'

The magpie flew off. Gwen relaxed. Telling Carter about the plague had taken all of her courage. He had just shrugged and squeezed her hand. And if he became ill...well, they would worry about that when it happened.

The petrol pump spluttered and stopped.

'Did you get enough?'

'Hope so.' Carter screwed the cap back onto the tank. 'Let's see if there's anything to eat.'

The gun was already in his hand as Gwen followed him towards the shop. She looked left and right, her heart rate increasing. Something was wrong.

She had the clearest feeling of being watched.

16

'Good evening, Prime Minister,' Madoc purred at the man on the huge screen in front of him. 'I hope you're feeling well?'

'Spare me the false small talk, John.'

Madoc studied the man's face. He looked tired and his skin was grey.

'As you wish,' Madoc replied. 'You've had enough time to consider?'

'It's not much of an offer. You get to run the country and in return the innocent people of the United Kingdom get this vaccine you're hoarding.'

'Just see it as another charitable donation, like the ones I've made to your political party over the years.' Madoc paused for maximum effect. 'And, of course, the donations I've made to your own pocket.'

The Prime Minister grew visibly paler.

'So it's blackmail, Madoc?'

'Yes, of course. Do you think I gave you all that money because I liked you? It was no more than an investment. Now it's time to collect.'

'I...I can't believe you're doing this. People are dying, Madoc. The country is in chaos. Have you no humanity?'

'Not really,' Madoc chuckled. 'So, to business. Dissolve Parliament. I know you can use emergency powers to appoint a special government. Do it, with me in charge. Then I want five billion pounds. When I get the money I'll release enough vaccine for you, your family and a few select friends. You decide who lives and who doesn't.'

'We'll use those vaccines to produce more,' the Prime Minister said. 'We can end this.'

'No, you can't. The doses have errors built into their genetic code. Any attempt to copy them will be unsuccessful. The real vaccine will be withheld until I am in control.'

'My God, what kind of monster are you?'

'Oh, you know. The kind of monster who holds the fate of millions in his hands. Not that dissimilar to you, really. You make unpleasant decisions every day, yes?'

'I don't kill people, Madoc.'

'That's because you're weak.'

The Prime Minister leaned closer to the screen. He looked beaten.

'You won't get away with this.'

'I already have. The police and army are ineffective. Nobody is coming to arrest me. Every minute that you hesitate, another thousand people fall sick. Six hundred of them will die. Tick tock, Prime Minister. Tick tock.'

'Damn you,' said the Prime Minister. His head dropped forwards. 'Your demands are met. You'll get your money, and a new government will be formed. I'll make sure you lead it.'

'Thank you,' Madoc said. 'You might just have saved many lives."

The screen blanked out. On the other side of the room, a fire blazed. Madoc took a remote control from his pocket. At the press of a button, a fierce jet of super-cooled gases erased the flames. The whole wall turned through ninety degrees, revealing a hidden room of dark shadows and red lights. An enormous round table hung from steel cables. It was painted exactly as the table in Winchester, with one significant difference. The king's face was unmistakeably John Madoc.

An ancient book rested on a plinth. Madoc lifted it up. It fell open at the page he wanted. He knew every word of the spell but it always gave him a special thrill to see it written down.

He imagined the scene at Bosworth Field as Henry Tudor's army swarmed around King Richard. He could see the swords and axes raining down on the king's head. And for an instant, his eyes glimpsed the book lying forgotten in the mud as his ancestor took it as his prize.

Madoc stared up at the painted king.

'We always knew another chance would come. And now it's time.'

***

The shop door was smashed open. They moved in, Carter first. His feet crunched against the broken glass. Sweat prickled across Gwen's forehead. If an attack came from outside they were already trapped. She felt the claustrophobia creep in, heightened by that nagging feeling of eyes on her.

Carter paused and listened, the gun held upright. He moved further into the shop. The smell of rotting food was strongest near the fridges. Water was pooled on the floor and the milk cartons had burst open to reveal thick blobs of curdled muck.

He motioned Gwen towards the chocolate bars and crisps before he disappeared behind one of the display stands. Instantly, a figure jumped out and dived after him.

'Gwen, run!' Carter yelled.

No way, she thought.

Gwen crouched low and sprinted forwards, remembering the hours of self-defence training. The attacker was sitting on Carter's chest, pinning him down by the wrists.

Gwen didn't hesitate. She delivered a crisp karate kick that knocked the man sideways. He fell away but recovered enough to lunge at Gwen. She was too quick for him. Her foot snaked out in a sharp roundhouse move and the man crashed into the wall. Gwen stepped forwards. A couple of sharp chops to the neck left him unconscious. It was over in five seconds. Carter scrambled to his feet, his eyes wide with shock.

'He came from nowhere. He coughed all over me.'

'It's sorted. Time to leave.'

She steered him towards the door, then she paused, grabbed a few bags of crisps and shoved them at Carter.

'Maybe he thought you weren't going to pay,' she said.

'Those were some serious moves you threw on him.'

'Forget it. Let's get out of here.'

They were soon back on the bike, heading west into Devon.

17

Madoc craned his neck to take in the whole of the Shard as it towered above him. The sun bounced off the acres of glass, hurting his eyes. His bodyguards and Randall stood a respectful distance away. The streets around them were deserted. People were hiding. People were scared.

Madoc strolled over to the doors of the visitor attraction called 'View from the Shard'. It was locked down and the lights were off. A sign had been hastily Sellotaped to the glass door.

CLOSED UNTIL FURTHER NOTICE

'Excuse me, sir.'

Randall had moved closer, interrupting his thoughts.

'What is it?'

'I think it's probably safer if we go back inside. I can't completely control the environment out here. Infected individuals might be unpredictable and dangerous. Some will have weapons.'

Randall was right, of course, but Madoc wanted to feel the sun on his face and the wind ruffling his hair. Inside the Shard, he was no better than a prisoner.

'Another few minutes,' Madoc said. 'Then we'll go back in. The latest news on my daughter, please.'

Randall glanced down at the tablet he carried everywhere.

'The GPS tracker in Gwendoline's watch gives her position close to Lynmouth.'

'Heading along the coastal road,' Madoc replied. 'Lundy island is a possibility.'

'Maybe. Perhaps too early to say, sir.'

'I can feel it all coming together.'

'Gabriel and his men will follow Gwendoline and the boy to wherever they're headed, sir.'

'Gabriel's your best?'

'I trained him myself, sir.'

'If it's Lundy, they'll need boats.'

'They have inflatables and outboard motors with them. The journey will be difficult but not beyond their abilities.'

'Sounds like you've thought of everything, Randall.'

'That's my job, sir.'

Madoc closed his eyes and turned his face to the sun, enjoying the faint warmth for a few more moments. It would have to be enough for now. It was time to go back inside. Randall and the silent bodyguards fell in behind him. The Shard swallowed them up, leaving the street deserted in the pale winter sunshine.

***

Gwen couldn't even begin to guess where they were. The miles slid by along deserted coast roads, then to Lynmouth and beyond, through deep ravines where towering wooded cliffs glared down at them. The motorbike struggled up the steep winding inclines. Hardly another vehicle passed by. People were staying at home. It was safer there. The rain was so heavy, Carter had to slow down to a crawl to avoid sliding off the road.

They were heading away from the sea and the worst of the wind, but the landscape opened up into endless fields with no cover. Gwen imagined a helicopter swooping down at them, her father's men leaning out ready to shoot. She gripped Carter's leathers more tightly and closed her eyes. She was exhausted but sleep was impossible. The road drifted back towards the coast. The salty rain hammered into them, raw and wounding, seeking out any patch of bare skin.

The weather eased as they made their way down into a town signposted as Woolacombe. Ahead, the sea and sky were the same blank grey – only the violent waves showed where one ended and the next began. They passed a small shop, closed and vandalised. The road took them into the heart of the town, a sad mix of boarded up restaurants and ice cream kiosks. Souvenir shops stood empty, a few discarded plastic buckets and spades scattered across the road. Carter slowed down the bike and they drifted to a halt. He pushed up the visor of his helmet and turned round to face Gwen.

'We're close. I can feel it.'

He scrambled down and ran across the deserted car park. Then he was on the sand, a tiny silhouette against the vast bleak expanse. Gwen followed him, calling his name. She felt utterly alone and exposed out here. What was she doing? Why had she believed what Carter had said? There was nothing here for them. Nothing at all.

'Where is it?' Carter screamed, his arms outstretched, whirling around looking for something that had no name, no shape, no substance.

He ran further out onto the beach, heading for the sea. The waves crashed down, a constant surging rush of foam and freezing spray. They had reached the end of the line. Gwen wanted to hold him and tell him it was all okay, they would find his island somewhere else. She trudged towards him, each step an enormous effort in the wet sand. She looked up as the scudding clouds parted. A shaft of weak sunlight picked out something on the horizon – a smudge of land.

'Carter, look there.'

He didn't answer her. He kept on whirling around, full of anger and frustration. She grabbed his shoulders and turned him to face the sea.

'There! An island, I know it is. That's it, Carter. Just like you said.'

'I was right.'

They stared in silence. The sunlight faded. The clouds closed over. The island disappeared from view as if it had never been there in the first place. Gwen sagged down onto her knees. She had no strength left.

'How the hell do we get there?' she asked.

'I...I don't know,' Carter said.

The island might as well have been a thousand miles away.

***

The Ravenmaster sat at his desk, a fresh mug of tea next to him. His eyes were red from lack of sleep. The radio kept repeating the same reports of how far the plague had spread, how the hospitals were overwhelmed, that the streets were deserted as people hid at home.

He turned it off then adjusted the heavy coat around his shoulders. It was cold in his office now that the heating had failed. There was a faint knock at the door.

'Come in.'

Another Yeoman Warder entered, his face gaunt.

'What is it, Mr Jarvis?' McKenna asked.

'You need to come and look at something, sir,' Jarvis said. He looked scared.

'Another raven dead?'

'No. Something else. It's Madeleine. She's acting...well, I know she's not normal, like, but this is something else.'

McKenna glared at the man.

'Watch what you're saying about her.'

'Sorry, Boss. That came out wrong. I don't really understand much about this Down's thing. Anyway, you'd better come and see.'

McKenna followed Jarvis outside. It was a clear night with a beautiful full moon. Their feet crunched on the icy steps which led up into the White Tower. Jarvis motioned him into the rooms of the Royal Armouries, the vast collection of weapons and armour that exhibited a thousand years of British history. Madeleine was huddled on the floor, slowly rocking backwards and forwards. Hug-a-Bug was clutched to her chest. Toffee wrappers were scattered around like autumn leaves.

'Ring a ring a roses,' she sang. 'Ring a ring a roses...ring a ring a ring a ring a ring...'

'She just keeps singing it,' Jarvis said. 'Same words again and again. Creepy.'

'You okay?' asked McKenna, kneeling down next to her. 'You should be in the canteen, darlin', not sitting here in the dark.'

Madeleine didn't answer. Instead, she pointed into the cabinet that held the armour of Edward of Woodstock, the Black Prince. A tiny gold sword was floating inside, a stunning amber jewel gleaming from the blade.

'What...how...'

Then Madeleine stood up and turned to face the Yeoman Warders. She blinked repeatedly, again and again. Again and again.

'Madeleine, you're scaring me. Say something.'

She dropped her ladybird and lifted a purple jewelled sword out of her jacket. The light from her eyes reflected in the precious stone and the gold.

'She's got one the same,' Jarvis whispered. 'Did you know that?'

'The lovely raven gave it me,' said Madeleine. 'He flew in here and told me it was mine. Oh, and mummy just died. That's made me a bit sad. But don't worry. The others will be here soon. I saw it all in my head.'

18

They sat quietly on the beach, lost in their own thoughts. Occasionally, a raven would call and swoop, then disappear into the inky blackness above. Luca closed his eyes, working through all he had seen and heard.

How could his entire world have changed so much? One minute he was in the hall, listening to that odd tour guide, then next he was here, wherever *here* was. It was enough to make him want to scream and run around in a blind panic, because he somehow felt he was already a different person from the one who had stared up at the round table, before it split in half and the madness began. He was...

'Still you,' Freddie murmured. 'You just know more, that's all. And you've got a cool sword.'

'Get out of my head,' Luca snarled. 'It's not yours to poke around in, okay?'

'He's right, Freddie,' said Jess. 'Try not to. I know you can do that.'

'Yeah. Sorry.'

Freddie looked away, his face dark with anger.

'He doesn't mean it,' Jess continued. Her voice cracked. 'This has all been a massive shock. I wish I could just be home now, with him and Josh. And mum and dad.'

'Yeah, wish I could be home as well. End of a regular day, boring school trip over, fish fingers and chips for tea.'

'My favourite,' Freddie whispered, still looking the other way.

He's just a kid, Luca thought. I need to give him a break.

'And mine. With a big glass of coke.'

A shy smile spread across Freddie's face.

'Chocolate afterwards. Always leave room for chocolate.'

'Always.'

Luca returned the smile, and glanced at Jess for approval. She nodded. That was enough. He looked away, trying to think of anything other than her, because sitting there with a kid who could read his mind was bad news, especially when it was his sister he was thinking about.

'So what do we do now? Just sit here like Peake said?'

'I think so,' Jess replied calmly. 'We wait for these others to arrive.'

'You said you've seen them.'

'Not much, to be honest. Just bits of them, like silhouettes. Two, travelling fast. I saw a city, London I think, and it looked like it was all falling apart. There was something else. I couldn't work it out. One of them seemed really scared, like escaping from there was the most important thing ever but leaving London was making her sad.'

'Her?'

'Yeah.' Jess rubbed her eyes. 'I'm sure one's a girl. I kind of recognised her, somehow. And that scared me. How could I know who she is?'

She smacked the sand.

'I hate it. I don't want to see stuff. I want to be normal.'

'You are,' Luca said, aware how pathetic that sounded. Surely he could come up with some really clever line, something to reassure and help her. He cursed inwardly.

'I think you're okay,' he whispered.

'Thanks, Luca. That means a lot.'

He swallowed, cheeks burning.

'Oh, please, you two,' groaned Freddie. 'This isn't the time for kissy kissy stuff. I want to know more about these swords and I want to go into Camelot. And I really want to know if there are any cool creatures in the lake.'

Thanks for the rescue, Luca thought, hoping Freddie would hear. Now I mean it - get out of there.

Freddie threw him a thumbs up.

'God, this is weird,' said Luca, shaking his head.

'Weird but kinda fun,' the younger boy laughed.

He was right, and Luca laughed with him, followed by Jess. Their laughter echoed along the beach and up the rocky walls, because the madness of it all was just too much. Luca laughed until his face hurt. It felt good after all they had been through. He thought about what Peake had said.

'The ravens at the Tower of London...do you know much about them? I was never any good at history stuff.'

'There are seven birds,' Freddie said, 'and they're always there. I remember learning about it in a school project we did. If the ravens leave the tower, people believe that Britain will be invaded or collapse or something like that. Sounded like a good story, that was all.'

Then lots of ravens dropped out of the darkness in huge numbers, hundreds of them, clattering and screaming, feathers flying into the air like black snow. Bran landed next to Luca, throwing sand over his chest and arms. He clicked his beak and swung his head upwards, as if pointing. He flapped heavily and was airborne, calling to the others. They rose as one, and in ten seconds it was all over. The children were alone again.

'What the hell was that about?'

'I think the others are here,' Jess said. 'I can feel them. And they're in for the ride of their lives.'

***

'We need to get to that island,' said Carter. 'I just know it.'

'There's no way there without a boat,' Gwen replied. 'It's miles away.'

Before Carter had a chance to answer, Gwen saw something that looked like a huge black cloud moving towards them at a speed that defied belief. It engulfed them and Gwen was thrown to the ground. Her eyes and nose were full of sand. She waved frantically at whatever it was that seemed to be attacking her.

'Crows!' Carter screamed.

No, thought Gwen, her skin crawling with fear and excitement. Ravens.

'Help me!'

Carter's voice was further away than she wanted it to be. He was lost in a swirling fog of birds. Then, and this made no more sense than anything else that had happened in the last two days, the sand seemed to be dropping away from her. Gwen dragged her feet down, trying to hang on to the beach as it sank.

A voice screamed in her head. Understand, it seemed to be saying. It's not the beach sinking. It's you that's rising up.

'I'm flying!' Gwen screamed.

The ravens dug their claws into her clothes to stop her getting away, and Gwen suddenly realised that even though she should have been terrified, she wasn't even remotely worried. It was the most exhilarating feeling, floating on a warm cushion of air. She closed her eyes and relaxed.

'Let them carry you,' she called to Carter, unsure if he could hear. The beat of the wings lulled her. Her head grew heavy. She was close to sleep.

A sudden sharp pain brought her back to her senses – a raven was pecking her ankle. The bird was flapping furiously, staring hatefully at her. Gwen kicked out and it flew away.

It seemed as if they flew for hours. Gwen looked down at the sea crashing against black cliffs. Was it the island? She had no way of knowing. Her view was obscured by beating wings. Carter could be next to her or ten miles away. Then without warning, she was hurtling down towards the waves.

'No!'

The ravens were still holding her, but she didn't feel secure in their grasp. She slipped and screamed, convinced she would fall. Then she was rising up again, this time along the cliff face. The rocks sped past at sickening speed. She thought she heard Carter calling. She had no strength left to respond.

Now the birds were heading directly for the cliffs. She closed her eyes, not wanting to see the moment of impact, hoping it would be quick and painless, but nothing happened. She risked a look. The wind was gone and she was suddenly warm and in darkness.

Gwen bumped against the sides of what might have been a tunnel. Then the ravens' hold on her was gone and she dropped like a stone, down and down, spinning around so she lost all sense of direction. She was aware of a soft glowing light and the echoing shrieks of the birds, then it was all over, because she was lying on soft sand.

'About time,' a young voice said from close by.

*****

Madoc's men stared out to sea. It was impossible, what they had just witnessed as they made their way down the steep hill into Woolacombe. How could two children float through the air on a cloud of birds?

Just thinking about it was enough to make them all fear for their sanity. Their weapons were held up ready to fire. They checked the sky for a possible attack.

Gabriel, their leader, moved to steady them, reminding them of their mission. Follow Mr Madoc's daughter and the boy. Identify their destination and then capture them. Nothing complicated, nothing difficult, especially for former special forces soldiers.

'We were warned there might be strange things here,' Gabriel said. 'Stay focused.'

He ordered them to get the inflatable boats out of the vans. The men's training kicked in as the shock of what they had seen faded. The boats were pushed forwards into the icy sea. Nothing would stop them.

19

Madoc's eyes flicked open. He was immediately awake. He glanced at the clock – nineteen minutes' sleep. No more than a nap but enough to brush away the fatigue.

'Randall,' he croaked into the intercom on his desk, 'I want an update.'

'Sir, there's been no change since I updated you last.' Randall's voice echoed through the office. 'And that was just twenty minutes ago.'

Madoc sensed the slightest hint of sarcasm. He was ready to explode into a rage but he stopped himself.

Keep calm, he thought. Stay strong. Stay in control.

Each of the office screens was still leading with the chaos engulfing Britain. He focused on the news in Canada.

'...absolutely disastrous,' a politician was saying, his tanned face fixed in a frown. 'It is not exaggerating the point when I say that Britain hasn't faced a threat like this since the days of the Black Death. The spread of this plague is creating an awful situation and we will do whatever we can to make sure it does not reach us.'

The man leaned forwards, looking directly at the screen. Madoc thought there was the hint of a tear in his eye.

'I just hope the British Government can deal with this before it all gets completely out of hand.'

Madoc flicked off the sound. The intercom buzzed.

'What is it?'

'The Prime Minister again, sir.'

'Tell him I'm busy.'

'Yes, sir.'

'Does he sound scared?'

'Very.'

'Good.'

'He begged for the vaccine, sir. His son might be showing signs of the plague.'

'Oh, that's a shame. Has the delivery left yet?'

'Awaiting your orders.'

'Keep him waiting a little longer.'

'Yes, sir.'

Madoc turned off the screens.

'Tell me again what Gabriel reported.'

'They were driving into Woolacombe. As they approached the beach a cloud of birds lifted Gwendoline and the boy into the air and carried them off to sea, towards Lundy island.'

Madoc closed his eyes, imagining that incredible scene.

'Definitely Merlin's work.'

'I can't think of another explanation, sir.'

'Is he hiding Camelot with some kind of spell? My satellites have photographed that coastline a thousand times.'

'I don't yet know.'

Madoc frowned. The lack of hard information was deeply annoying. He thought of Gwendoline, the anger rising in him like lava. She had gone against him, leaving the safety and security of the world he had built for her. She was a traitor. Why else was she travelling with the boy?

Madoc reached inside his shirt and took out a sword. The blade was black. A diamond skull grinned from the hilt.

'The other twelve will be mine,' he whispered.

'Are you still there, Mr Madoc?'

It was Randall's voice, crackling through the intercom.

'Yes. Inform me as soon as you know anything.'

'Of course, sir. Your family has waited a long time for this.'

'A long time? Centuries, Randall. Centuries! And soon the *true* Pendragon will be king.'

***

Gwen brushed herself down, looked around and stifled a gasp at what she saw. A beach, a lake and a castle that seemed to be part of the endless looming rocks. She felt sick and dizzy, which was hardly surprising considering the ride she and Carter had just experienced. Ravens swooped and called above, black dots in the distance, impossibly high. And there were three children staring at them. A strange glowing light like milky mist softened their faces, but not enough to hide the dark anger that glared from the eyes of the youngest. She tried a smile, hoping it would break the tension. She looked away. She had the weirdest sensation in her brain, as if a tiny insect was scuttling around inside.

'Who are you?' Carter asked. His voice was cracked and strained. His gun was pointing towards the children.

'I'm Luca Broom,' the older boy said, holding out a hand for Carter to shake. Carter ignored the friendly gesture.

'My name's Jess,' added the girl. 'This is my brother, Freddie.'

Gwen blinked. That feeling was still nagging away in her head. For a moment, she imagined that the younger boy could see what she was thinking. That was so crazy, she almost laughed out loud. Gwen decided to take control of the situation - she had spent enough years ordering staff around to know how to gain the upper hand. She stepped forwards so that she was in front of Carter.

'He'll shoot you if I tell him to.'

'No he won't,' the girl said. There was the faintest of smiles on her face. Gwen realised the girl wasn't scared.

'I saw you coming in here.'

Jess pointed at her forehead.

'Can we trust them?' the friendly boy asked.

'I think so,' said the girl.

Carter was silent. His hand was shaking slightly. One wrong move and there might be an accident. She placed her hand on the barrel of the weapon and gently pushed Carter's arm down.

'I'm Gwen,' she said in the strongest voice she could manage. 'He's Carter.'

'You don't need that,' said Jess, looking at the gun.

'Show us your swords,' the younger boy said.

Something was happening in the dark shadows behind the children, a disturbance of some sort. Dozens of ravens flew down and began circling, like vultures over a kill. And Gwen's heart hammered loudly in her chest, because the young boy was staring at her like he wanted to rip it out and laugh as he did so.

20

Luca sized up the newcomers. The one called Carter had a gun and seemed ready to use it. The posh girl with the pretty face and the snobby voice was scared stiff. He glanced at the others. Jess was calm as usual. Freddie had murder on his mind.

'It's all right,' he said, probably to everybody there. 'You're safe.'

'You don't have a sword,' Freddie said. 'I was in your head. Do you know that my mum and dad are dead?'

Luca was shocked at the anger in the boy's voice. Nobody spoke. The silence was broken by the sound of footsteps. Peake was crossing the stones towards them. He had aged, and walked with a limp. His skin was grey in the milky light and there were dark smudges under his eyes. A flurry of ravens swooped around him. Bran settled down on the sand next to Luca. He reached down and rubbed Bran's head like a shepherd greeting his dog.

'Sorry I'm so slow,' Peake said as he made his way up the beach. 'Welcome to Camelot.'

Peake lifted a hand. The gun flew away from Carter and landed on the sand between them.

'No need for that here, son.'

Carter's eyes were fixed on the weapon.

'How did you do that?'

111

'Magic,' murmured Freddie, his face still a mask of fury.

Peake chuckled.

'Step forwards, the pair of you. Introduce yourselves.'

Carter and Gwen exchanged glances. Carter shrugged and moved out of the shadows, his hand in Gwen's.

'My name's Carter,' he said. His voice was strong. 'I'm from London. I saw you lot in a dream. You were telling me to go west and find you. So here I am. And here's our sword.'

He held it up. Luca leaned in closer to look.

'Hands off,' said Carter, his eyes narrow and hard.

'No problem,' Luca replied, backing away. 'Just trying to be friendly.'

'I thought so,' whispered Peake, moving between them as he stared at the sword. 'Brave, no doubt. I don't suppose you think about things too deeply. Simple is best. You just go with your guts, eh?'

'Who you calling simple, old man?' Carter growled. He looked ready for a fight. Peake bowed slightly.

'No offence meant, son. A simple approach is usually the best. I've never been fond of people who are too clever. I reckon you'll do just fine.'

'Why are we here?' Carter asked. He didn't sound altogether convinced that he hadn't just been insulted. 'And how does that stuff with the birds work? They carried us over the sea and then down here. That's just too weird.'

'The ravens wouldn't think of flying as weird,' Peake replied. He turned his attention to Gwen. 'And you, young lady. Move forwards. I can't see you clearly back there.'

Gwen hesitated. Luca watched her reach for her neck, as if she was willing there to be a sword there. He saw a flash of metal and diamonds on her wrist. She was wearing the most incredible watch he had ever seen.

'I don't think you told us your name,' Peake continued in a quiet voice. Luca's mouth was suddenly dry. It was something about the way Peake spoke. There was no warmth there, no welcome. And Freddie still looked like he was ready to kill somebody.

'Gwen,' she whispered.

'Do you have another name, Gwen?'

'Leave her alone,' Carter warned. 'You're scaring her.'

'I know what it is,' Freddie said. 'I know all about her.'

'That's enough,' said Peake. 'It's a simple question. Your surname, please.'

Gwen stood up. She was breathing hard, her eyes bright with fear.

'It's Madoc.'

'I knew it!' shouted Freddie as dozens of ravens immediately plummeted down.

Carter swung his arms around to fight off the attack. Luca joined him, angry at what was happening. Gwen looked like a frightened kid, not a killer. Peake stood in silent contemplation, his head cocked to one side. The dive-bombing continued. One of the ravens managed to snag Gwen's hair and she screamed. That was enough for Peake. He clapped his hands together. The assault carried on for a moment until he clapped again.

'Stop,' he shouted.

The ravens flew off into the darkness, leaving only Bran still on the sand.

'Well, this is interesting,' Peake said. 'We've clearly got a lot to talk about.'

***

Above ground, Madoc's men staggered up out of the swirling waters as their boats were smashed to pieces on the razor sharp rocks of Lundy.

Gabriel held up his GPS tracker whilst his men sorted through their kit and checked their weapons. The signal from Gwen's watch beeped. Moving steadily in spite of the cold and fatigue, the men headed up onto a path. They marched in silence for an hour before Gabriel gave the order to start searching by torchlight.

'Come and look at this,' one of the men said after a few minutes.

The tracker gave out a constant signal. Gabriel bent down and grabbed a handful of black feathers mixed up in the mud and grass of a cliff edge. He turned to his men.

'Time to abseil.'

***

The Ravenmaster guided Madeleine into the canteen. The Warders tried not to stare at Madeleine but it was impossible. They sat in silence, waiting for McKenna to speak. He cleared his throat.

'Most of you have known Madeleine since she was a little kid,' he said. 'As far as I'm concerned, she's as normal as the rest of us. She might look a bit different, and be a bit slower on the uptake, but that doesn't count for anything in my book. I know at least a dozen of you still take a teddy to bed with you.'

That raised a few laughs. He pressed on.

'So, the first one to say anything bad about her can repeat it to me outside. Understand?'

Nobody spoke.

'Good. Now, there's some weird stuff going on here. Deal with it. We're all experienced soldiers. We're used to challenging situations. This is just another one. I heard what she said about talking ravens and kids coming here. So did Jarvis. And you've all seen the sword in the cabinet. I don't know what it means any more than you do, but it's real enough. She's got one, too.'

He paused, letting his words sink in.

'Madeleine says these kids are going to have swords as well. It's something to do with the bird plague and our ravens. Don't any of you look at me funny because I know how this sounds. When these other children arrive we need to help them because the ravens are dying. Crazy? You bet. Do I believe it? I've got no reason not to.'

A low murmur rippled through the canteen as they muttered to each other. McKenna looked around at his colleagues. He smiled.

'Make no mistake - we've been lucky. Nobody's caught the plague yet. We've done what we thought was the right thing by staying to guard the Tower. I've also made it clear if you feel you should go then I won't stop you. Your families are out there. That still stands, but I intend to wait for these kids. I've got a bit bored with playing at it. I'd quite like to be a soldier again.'

'With you, sir,' one called.

'Try and stop us,' shouted another.

'We're not leaving you to get all the medals, boss!'

More voices, louder, then clapping, and the whole canteen roaring with the sound of comrades eager for one more mission.

Madeleine pushed back the hood of her coat. Fiery red hair tumbled around her shoulders and she held up her sword.

'I'll protect you, if you believe.' Then she grinned at McKenna. 'Can I have a toffee, uncle Sam?'

Suddenly, the door flew open and Jarvis burst in. His face was full of pain.

'I've come from the aviary. Another raven's dead.'

21

The ropes swung wildly in the ferocious storm. The men on the end of them struggled to maintain any sort of control. They were going down blind without any knowledge of the cliff face. There could be vicious snags of rock that would slice skin and muscle in a second. There might be an ambush waiting for them.

'Keep them still,' Gabriel ordered the men straining to help their dangling colleagues. They pulled harder until the lines were steadied. They lowered the men another five metres, then another ten. Any more and they would be in the sea.

Then came a shout from below. Gabriel moved closer to the edge, straining to hear what was being said.

'A tunnel system, boss! It's small, but we can just get in. Ravens everywhere!'

'Can you see the end?'

'No. Dark as hell. Gonna be a long climb down.'

'That's it,' he said to the rest of his team. 'Fasten off the ropes and get your own attached to something. I want us all in that tunnel five minutes from now.'

A raven flew past him, buffeted by the wind. Gabriel swiped at it with a gloved hand. The raven came again. This time he pulled out his pistol and shot the bird at point blank rage. Feathers and blood exploded everywhere. He prepared to abseil over the cliff. Madoc's men were heading in.

***

Gwen's head swam with the sights and smells of it all. Her skin burned from the ravens' claws. Her heart banged in her chest. The boy called Freddie was glaring at her.

'Your dad made the plague. He killed my dad. And my mum. And my baby brother's probably going to die any day now. I hate you.'

'Freddie,' said Peake without looking at him, 'I don't think she played a part in any of that.'

He glanced at Gwen but she said nothing. Peake spoke again, saving her from the silence.

'I'm going to tell Gwen and Carter everything that you others already know. Then they'll tell us their story. That's the way it's going to be. If anybody disagrees, leave now. The ravens will take you back to the mainland. No? Good. Now listen.'

***

'You've all heard it now,' Peake said. 'We don't have a lot of time. The plague's spreading quickly, from what Gwen and Carter have told us. They've done well to get here. Passed their test, yeah?'

Luca nodded, Bran was next to him, rubbing his head against his leg.

'He really does like you,' Jess whispered.

And Luca felt a wave of odd affection for the raven. He grinned at Jess, blushing because she held his gaze for just a second too long.

'Get over the anger about Miss Madoc,' continued Peake. 'She's not responsible for the crimes of her father. There are twelve swords of Camelot and so there must be twelve children. The ravens decide when they're needed, not me. The last time was during World War Two. Those youngsters were incredibly brave but of course nobody knows anything about them because it's all top secret. Not even the Prime Minister has any idea.'

Luca glanced up at Camelot, brooding over them like a breaking storm. Peake had said they would need to go in there. He wanted to go now, to find out all he could. He had never felt more alive and excited.

'Your ancestors were the knights Gawain and Percival,' Peake said, pointing at Jess and Freddie. 'You're wearing their swords. And you, Carter, you're the last descendent of Sir Lancelot.'

His words hung in the air, the meaning sinking in. Suddenly, this all felt a lot more ominous.

'I'm afraid I don't have any good news for you, Gwen. Your ancestor chose a different path, but the ravens have brought you here so you have a part to play in all this.'

Gwen nodded, her eyes narrow and determined. Luca waited, his heart rate increasing. What would Peake tell him?

'And you, Luca Broom,' the old man said, 'you're a very special boy. The broom plant in Latin is *Planta genista*. Sound familiar?'

A sudden memory tugged at Luca's brain.

'Plantagenet. The guide said it, on my school trip.'

'Correct. Rulers of Britain for more than three hundred years.'

Peake pointed at Luca's sword.

'That can only be worn by the Pendragon, the true monarch. You're the last living descendent of Arthur, King of the Britons.'

Luca felt Jess's hand touch his.

'This is really happening, right?' he asked.

'Yes.'

Luca turned to Peake.

'Tell me what that means.'

'Good lad. When you were born, I went to see your mum and dad. They struggled with it, of course. Your dad wouldn't believe a word. He was a soldier, a man of action. He had no time for an idiot on his doorstep talking about knights and magic.'

'You came to my house?'

'Yes, on the army base where you lived before...well, when it was the three of you.'

A sharp pain stabbed at Luca's chest. He remembered the small garden, kicking a ball with his dad, and being the happiest it was possible to be.

'I showed them what I was. They believed then.'

'I miss them,' Luca whispered.

'They'd be proud of you right now,' Peake replied.

'Mum would want to know if I had clean socks on. And dad would be cracking bad jokes.'

'We all know how you feel, mate,' Carter said. 'Anything we can do, just shout, yeah?'

'Thanks. It helps having you lot here. And I know it's not just me that's missing somebody.'

Luca took out the crumpled photograph and read out his dad's words.

'Incredible things are going to happen. Be ready. Be smart. Believe, and follow your heart. It will always take you to the right place.'

His voice cracked. Don't cry now, he thought. Not now, when everybody's staring.

He tried to read again but his voice faltered.

'I love you so much, my amazing boy,' said Jess, finishing it. 'That's what he wrote. And I know he would say exactly the same thing if he was here with us now.'

'He kept all of this from me. So did mum. Why?'

'To protect you,' Peake said. 'You didn't need to know. And you've looked after your mum since your dad died.'

Luca's cheeks burned.

'I did what I had to do.'

'You certainly did. And you're going to have do a lot more. The blood of kings is in your veins. The children of Camelot have been called. The ravens at the Tower of London are dying and that can't happen. Britain will fall and Madoc will take over. You've all got to stop him.'

'Us? A bunch of kids? Impossible.'

'Not a word I know, Luca. You've got the swords, and inside Camelot you'll find a way to make them work for you. Time to go inside your castle, Pendragon.'

'I don't feel much like a leader,' Luca said.

'Bran gave you the sword.'

'How did I end up here?'

'Humility is good. Doubt, less so. Embrace your destiny, son. And the rest of you.'

Suddenly, without warning, Jess fell forwards, holding her head.

'No,' she gasped. 'I can see...coming...close...too close...here!'

'What's going on?' Carter asked.

'She's seeing the future,' said Freddie. 'Except I think this is nearly the present.'

Jess's eyes flickered left and right.

'Men with guns,' Jess said. Her voice was cracked, like feet crunching over broken glass.

From somewhere high above them, Luca heard the unmistakeable rattle of gunfire.

***

Randall entered the office.

'News, please,' said Madoc.

'Gabriel has found a way in, sir.'

'So Camelot is underground.'

'His last message stated that they were making their way through a tunnel system. A well-hidden place, accessible only by abseiling. He's found a shaft that opens up into a huge cavern. I ordered him to go straight in before the signal was lost.'

'This is it, Randall.' Madoc whispered. 'And Gwendoline?'

'She must be down there with the others.'

'I should be there, not stuck here like a rat in a cage.'

'Once Camelot is secured you can go whenever you want.'

'Imagine Merlin's face when he realises his pathetic attempt to stop me has failed.'

Madoc glanced at his tablet he carried. Four lights were red – four ravens dead.

22

'We've run out of time!'

Peake's voice cut through the gunfire. Luca saw the muzzle flashes and instinctively ducked down. Black shapes were dropping from above.

'Everybody okay?' he shouted, but they were too busy avoiding being shot to respond.

'Madoc's boys,' gasped Carter. 'Gwen said he wouldn't give up.'

He grabbed Luca's sleeve.

'I've seen them up close. They don't take prisoners.'

Luca hesitated, unsure what to do.

'Spread out,' Peake urged. 'Don't bunch up.'

Bran flitted around their heads, urgently screeching and clacking. The men were getting closer to the ground. They would land on the beach about a hundred metres away. One man released his rope too soon. He fell twenty metres into the water and did not surface.

The next ones fared better. They released at the right moment, landing awkwardly but at least on dry land. They were calling to each other, trying to organise themselves.

'Get into Camelot,' said Peake. 'I'll do what I can out here.'

Four men had increased to twelve. More were falling by the second. They were up against a small army. Gwen and Carter were already moving. Freddie was urging Jess to her feet. She seemed a bit dazed. Luca helped and together they encouraged her to walk down to the stones. Luca knew it was too far. The men would be on them in no time.

Loud hissing filled the air. Smoke grenades began to billow out all around them just as masses of ravens swooped down from the cliff heights. They passed through the smoke like wraiths and fell onto the men. The advance was slowed for a moment but a burst of fire blew the birds apart. They continued forwards through a cloud of pink blood and floating feathers.

'Go, go, go!' Peake yelled, bundling them along. He looked scared and that was not good. 'Past the statues. There's an archway and a door. Then keep running. You'll find a hall. Arthur's round table is there. Use it to activate your swords. Go!'

He closed his eyes and spread his arms out. A low boom shuddered through the sand and he turned into a huge ball of light. The ball spread out, picking up speed and expanding all the time. Their attackers were thrown back by it, limbs splayed, shouts muffled. The light died away. Peake hunched over, hands on his knees, breathing heavily. The magic had exhausted him, but it had bought them a few precious seconds.

Luca felt one of the ravens brush past. Sharp claws snagged into his clothes and he knew it was Bran. The huge bird was trying to drag him along all by himself.

'Come on! Do as Peake says!'

They half-dragged, half-carried Jess between them. They ran as one, feet echoing against the stones. The other side was tantalisingly close, the statues emerging out of the gloom, then Luca paused and turned. Peake was not following them. He stood motionless on the beach, facing the onrushing men.

'What are you doing?' Luca shouted.

'Keep going, son. Get into the castle.'

'No!'

Peake glanced over his shoulder. He suddenly looked ancient, but he smiled and his eyes were still young.

'You'll be fine. I know you will. All of you.'

'Come on,' Luca urged him. 'They're getting closer.'

'It has to be this way.'

'But I don't know what to do! I don't know anything!'

'Love, friendship and belief, Luca. That's all you need to know.'

Peake started to change into something that wasn't even human. His body stretched impossibly, like melting rubber. Smoke and steam poured out of him, and in an instant Peake was gone. In his place, four animals crouched in a snarling mass of teeth and claws – a giant wolf, an eagle, a dragon and the bear.

'I don't know what's going on, Carter said, 'but this is our chance.'

At that moment Luca hated him, but he knew Carter was right. They had to go. Luca jumped down onto the beach. The sand slowed them down, and his leg muscles quickly burned with the effort of trudging forwards. The statues loomed over them.

'Arthur and his men,' Freddie said, as if they were on a day trip.

'Lovely,' grunted Carter. 'Remind me to buy a guide book next time.'

As Luca made his way through the circle, he wished they would come to life like before and attack the men, but the statues remained cold and impassive. He saw the archway that Peake had described. A closed wooden door blocked the way into Camelot.

If that's locked, he thought, this will all be over really quickly.

A circle was carved into the stones above it, divided into segments, each one etched with a sign of the zodiac. It reminded Luca of the table in the Winchester hall, where all of this had begun.

A bullet thudded into the door, then another, each one flying past with a high pitched whistle. Each hit left a pale scar in the wood. They started to run, calling each other on. Luca ducked and swerved, gasping for breath, his legs jellied with terror.

The next explosion of gunfire came from somewhere very close. Luca glanced back and saw that Freddie had picked up a discarded machine gun. He was emptying it towards the men.

'Get through the archway,' Freddie shouted, his focus on their attackers. He fired again and again.

One of the men lunged at Luca. Bloody claw marks were slashed across his cheek. He flicked up his gun, ready to fire, and Luca knew that he was about to die. A blur of movement came from his left. It was Gwen in a spiralling dance of kicks and chops. The man collapsed onto the sand.

'Wow,' said Luca.

Jess was screaming, trying to get to Freddie, but there was no way back. There were too many of them swarming around. Carter pulled her towards the door. Freddie was down on one knee, his head and shoulders wreathed in gun smoke like a cowboy in a western. It all seemed to be happening in slow motion. He had dropped his sword. It glittered against the dark sand. Luca grabbed it and started forwards, but he had to give up because the boy was cut off from them, surrounded by Madoc's men. Ravens pelted down like missiles and for a second it looked like Freddie might have a way through, but the men closed around him again. The animals that had emerged from Peake were still battling, but even they were in desperate trouble. Luca watched the dragon and eagle plummet down into the lake and explode in flames, shot to pieces.

The wolf howled one last time, blood dripping from his fangs. Mangled bodies lay next to him. Then a volley of bullets tore it apart and it faded away to nothing, leaving just the bear. It dived into the mass of men crossing the stones. It scooped up six of them and fell into the lake. Sparks and flames shot out in all directions. A cloud of hissing steam mushroomed up into the air. Ravens were everywhere, blocking his view, forcing him against the door. He was just aware of Carter wrenching it open, then they fell into Camelot, leaving Freddie behind in the noise and chaos.

23

'They're still coming,' shouted Carter, slamming shut another door. Every twist and turn led them deeper through the castle. Gwen was in front, dragging Jess with her. The girl struggled hard but there was less effort than before.

Freddie saved us, Luca thought, the boy's sword held tightly in his fist. And now he's probably dead.

'Did I really see all that stuff with the animals?' Carter asked as they ran.

Luca nodded, unable to speak.

'A real dragon. That's the weirdest thing yet. So, where do we go? Those doors won't hold 'em for long.'

Luca slowed down. His brain wasn't working. Nothing made sense. Carter grabbed his shoulders.

'Come on! Where do we go?'

Luca blinked, trying to think clearly.

'We can't leave Freddie,' he said.

'Freddie saved our necks. So let's make sure he didn't do that for nothing. Where do we go?'

'Peake said something about a hall, and a table that will make the swords work.'

'Then that's what we look for.'

Carter was calm, his eyes cold. Luca wanted to hit him.

'Luca,' Carter said, 'going back is suicide.'

'He's right,' added Jess. She was pale in the strange light of the tunnel, and her hands trembled, but she looked at Luca with an intensity that made his skin tingle. 'I abandoned him. He's all I've got left.'

'You had no choice,' Luca said. 'None of us did. We'll find him, okay? I promise you, we'll find him.'

The words were out even before Luca knew what he was saying.

'You promise me?'

Luca nodded.

'Reach out to him with your mind. Tell him we won't leave him.'

Jess carried on staring. Her breathing was rapid and Luca guessed she might be going into shock. He took her palm and wrapped her fingers around Freddie's sword.

'Do it, Jess. I know you can. Tell him!'

She blinked and then closed her eyes. She was getting herself back under control. She scrunched up her face, concentrating hard. Precious seconds passed by.

Come on, Luca thought. Tell me he's all right.

'He's still alive!' Jess shouted. 'I can feel him!'

'That's all I need to hear. Now we have to go.'

'Okay.'

Luca turned away. He didn't want Jess to see the doubt written across his face like a neon sign. They carried on through the maze of corridors and tunnels.

Up ahead, at the end of a long straight incline, two huge doors stood shut, barring their way.

'That has to be it,' Carter said.

He sprinted up to the doors and turned the iron handles. They moved easily without a sound. The others gathered around him, waiting. He took a deep breath and pushed. The doors wouldn't budge.

'Too heavy. Help me.'

Even with all their combined strength there wasn't enough space to squeeze through. They tried again, and just when they were ready to give up, the doors seemed to take on a life of their own. They swung inwards as if on springs.

'Everybody in.'

Luca didn't know if he had led them into a dead-end. At that moment he didn't know much of anything. They moved through into the semi-darkness, feeling their way with outstretched hands. The light began to build, revealing the scale of the place. Luca froze, barely able to believe what he was seeing. The hall was the size of a football pitch. The walls ran straight up to a dazzling white ceiling made up of what looked like interlocking bones. Long tapestries hung down. Each one was embroidered with the stern face of a knight. A blackened fireplace was at the far end and the longest tapestry hung above it, showing a bearded man with piercing blue eyes and a thin gold crown.

'King Arthur,' Luca whispered.

'And I reckon that's the table,' Carter answered, pointing at the floor.

A huge circle was carved into the granite slabs, and the circle was divided into twelve segments just like the one over the archway. A different symbol had been gouged into each one.

'The zodiac,' Jess said.

Luca touched the stone. His fingers prickled as if it was charged with static. He traced the outline of two fish. Pisces, his birth sign.

Peake said the table would make the swords work, he thought.

He touched the blade against the symbol. Immediately, it began to glow red hot. Millions of tiny lights flashed inside the diamond. Voices whispered off the walls, like wind passing through winter trees. A sudden vision of the red-haired girl flashed through his brain. She was calling to him, and there were ravens all around her.

'This is where all the magic comes from,' Luca said.

But even as he spoke, Gwen cried out in pain. She clutched at her throat. Her lips turned blue. Her eyes bulged. Then she collapsed, still as a corpse.

24

McKenna wrapped his cloak around Madeleine's shoulders. The cold was biting up there on the ramparts. He looked out across London.

'Lots of fires, uncle Sam.'

'I know, darlin'. Bit like bonfire night.'

'Yes, but I think these are bad fires, don't you?'

He nodded in the darkness.

'Yeah. Gas pipes and electric wires shorting out, I reckon. And no fire brigade to help.'

'I think all the shouting we can hear is people feeling very sad about the plague,' she whispered.

He remained silent, eyes fixed on the shadowy outlines of buildings silhouetted against an ominous glowing sky. The city was falling apart. Madeleine squeezed his hand.

'It will be okay once the others get here.'

'I wish they would hurry up.'

'They can't, silly. They're stuck.'

He looked down at her.

'What does that mean?'

'I saw it in my head. A big cave and a lake. A castle like this one, but better. And men with guns. Not nice ones like you and the other soldiers. Nasty men. Trying to shoot them.'

'When did you see this?'

'Just now. I could see it all. And the ravens were talking lots. In fact, they were really shouting.'

He shook his head. 'This is freaky stuff, Madeleine.'

'Well, the ravens sound perfectly normal to me.'

She wrinkled her nose at him, as if chatting with birds was something everybody should be able to do.

'If these kids are stuck we're in trouble.'

'Maybe. Maybe not. I told them to come here as soon as they can.'

'Did they hear you?'

'I hope the boy did. I'll keep trying.'

McKenna crouched down so that his face was level with hers.

'This boy who you say is some kind of king?'

'Yes. He's nice, but I think he's sad too. I think his mummy is poorly.'

'Well, if they can get here, me and the boys will help any way we can. Tell him that, eh?'

'Already have. I would really like another toffee.'

He smiled.

'I think you've had enough, love.'

'Maybe one for Hug-a-Bug?'

'Nice try. Come on, let's go back inside. It's freezing out here.'

The steps down were icy and he held her hand until they were safely on the gravel outside the White Tower. He heard the ravens chattering in their aviary.

'Noisy tonight.'

Madeleine suddenly stopped, her head cocked to one side as if she was listening to something, or someone.

'What is it?' McKenna asked.

'Not just our ravens,' she answered. When she turned to look at him, her eyes shone as the tears flowed. 'The bad men have killed lots of them there, too.'

'At this other castle?'

'Yes.'

'I think I need a mug of tea and some of your toffees. Let's share them.'

He led her across the grounds to the staff quarters, and across London fires raged and people died.

25

'Help me!' Carter shouted. 'What's wrong with her?'

Gwen lay curled on the floor, unconscious and barely breathing.

'I don't know,' Luca said.

'It was when you put your sword on the table. Something happened and then she just fell over.'

'I didn't do anything.'

'Stop arguing,' interrupted Jess. 'We can worry about what and how later. The men are coming.'

Luca heard the echo of footsteps and the soft murmur of voices.

'Shut the doors,' Luca said.

Carter grabbed his shoulders.

'Help Gwen!'

'If we don't shut the doors we're all dead.'

Jess checked Gwen's pulse.

'She's alive. Now do as Luca says.'

'They weigh a ton,' grunted Carter. 'We only just managed to open them.'

They dragged Gwen out of sight. The men's footsteps were growing louder.

'We've had it,' Carter said.

Luca closed his eyes, thinking about what Peake had said and the power he had felt as the sword had touched the stone symbol.

Think...think...

Finian Black

Every problem has a solution. The problem was the doors. They were too heavy to push.

'We need a bloody miracle,' Carter yelled.

Bullets smashed into the doorway. Luca flinched as they were showered with stone fragments. More shots. Dust and smoke all around them.

'No,' Luca answered. 'We need magic.'

He jumped up.

'Carter, you've got to do what I did.'

Carter didn't move.

'Your sword, mate. It's got to be woken up, or whatever that was. And Jess's, and Freddie's as well.'

'Why?' Jess asked.

'Because of the power they'll have. Don't ask me how I know. I just do.'

'They can see straight into the hall. I don't know if we can make it without being shot.'

Carter shrugged.

'Let's find out. Here goes nothing.'

He crouched down and sprinted out across the floor. He rolled onto the carvings.

'First of August,' he shouted, slamming his sword down. 'Leo the bloody lion.'

The blade glowed hot. He scrambled to his feet and dived to safety.

'It feels like I could take on a whole army,' he gasped, holding the sword up. 'And I saw...I don't know what it was. A girl?'

'Yeah.'

138

Luca looked at Jess.

'You've got to do the same.'

She held out the swords.

'Taurus for me, Gemini for Freddie. I can do this.'

'Be careful,' Luca said. 'They're so close.'

'Back in no time.'

She sprinted away. Luca risked a look down the tunnel. The men were moving forwards in pairs, weapons up and ready. Then he saw a small pale face, just visible in the darkness – Freddie.

Jess had made it. First one, then two blades glowed red hot. She stood up, took a deep breath and made her way back.

'That was easy,' she grinned, but her eyes betrayed the fear. 'Now what?'

'Let them touch.'

He showed them what he meant. As the blade tips approached, Luca felt a surge of immense power building in the handle. He struggled to keep the sword still. Carter was shouting but Luca couldn't hear what he was saying. A dazzling white light exploded around them. It was as if the swords were suddenly ten times larger, like full-sized weapons ready for battle.

'Don't let go!' Luca screamed.

The light split apart into a stunning rainbow of colour. Red merged into orange, yellow, green and then deepest blue, wrapping around the doors like huge hands. In an instant they slammed shut. Luca collapsed, exhausted. The light was gone.

'We did it,' Jess said.

'Yeah,' Carter replied. 'We did something. That was crazy. Did you feel the power? I thought my hand was going to explode.'

'They'll try to blast their way through,' Luca said, 'but I don't think it'll be that easy.'

Dull thuds hammered at the doors like lethal rain.

'Now you help me with Gwen,' Carter said.

There was still a faint pulse, but Luca didn't like the blue tinge her lips or the way her eyelids fluttered. There was something badly wrong with her. He felt completely helpless.

'We need to get her out of this hall,' said Jess. 'She isn't like us, don't you see? She doesn't have a sword. She's...she's a Madoc.'

'So?'

'So maybe there's some kind of curse here, and the swords are part of it. You felt what they can do. This whole place is full of magic. We don't know a millionth of it.'

Carter's mouth opened and closed like a goldfish.

'I think Jess might be right,' Luca said. 'Just accept it for now, okay?'

'I'm going to have to. You promise me she'll be all right if we move her from here?'

Luca nodded, aware he was making another promise he had no idea he could keep.

'Okay then,' Carter said, 'let's find a way out.'

***

The production line was deep within the Shard, windowless and sealed to protect against accidental contamination. The virus might have been buried for two thousand years but it was just as potent as ever. The horrible deaths of the workmen who uncovered it proved that.

Madoc stared through the thick glass windows as his scientists worked in silence, their faces hidden behind masks, their bodies completely covered by white overalls. The air cleaning system hummed gently somewhere above him.

'Did you really believe we could do it, Randall?' he asked.

'Of course, sir,' Randall replied. 'You planned every detail, every eventuality.'

'Did I?'

'I believe so, yes.'

'Then why do I feel a nagging doubt I'm missing something?'

Randall paused, his face impassive.

'Perhaps because of the Gwendoline situation.'

'That's one way of describing it,' Madoc said darkly. 'It's taking too long. What the hell is going on down there?'

'Gabriel is my best man, sir. He will be securing the site. Once he can contact us, he will.'

Madoc went back to staring at the production line. Thousands of vials of vaccine trundled past on polished rollers, ready to be packed into polystyrene boxes.

'He never imagined I would locate the virus,' he whispered. 'He thought it was safe, so far underground.'

'He doesn't know you have his book, sir.'

'No. And of course, only someone of my intellect would be able to work out the clues.'

Randall nodded.

'It won't be long before all the ravens are dead. Then we can go to the Tower.'

'Will I have some of the swords soon, Randall?'

'I cannot answer that, Mr Madoc.'

'My family has waited a lot of years. I can wait a while longer.'

26

'Let's carry her over there,' Luca said, pointing at the fireplace on the opposite side of the hall, as far from the door as we can get. 'They'll be through soon. We need to find another way out of here.'

'What if there isn't one?' Carter asked, lifting Gwen's arms.

'There has to be,' replied Luca, taking Gwen's ankles.

'Careful with her, yeah?'

'We're all on the same side, Carter. Chill out a bit. Oh, and that was seriously brave, running out to the table. You could have been shot.'

Carter's face softened.

'Well...thanks. Same with you, Jess. And the sword thing was a great idea. So, I guess we're all brilliant. One each.'

Luca grinned. He already liked Carter. He was straight to the point, funny and completely unaware of danger. And he clearly adored Gwen.

'Yeah. Superheroes, aren't we?'

'Actually,' Jess said, as they carried Jess to the fireplace, 'I suppose we kind of are. We've got the swords. And when I saw the girl with the red hair, I felt like...' She paused, looking for the right words. 'I felt like I could reach through anything to get to her. I felt really special.'

She blushed and looked away.

'I felt it too,' said Carter. 'And I'm only here because you called out to me, so I'm with you, Jess. Superheroes we are. Just don't ask me to put on a costume, okay?'

They laughed at that, a sudden release of humour after the tension. And Freddie was still alive, which meant that at least one of Luca's promises could still be kept. They placed Gwen down. She was cool and pale, her breathing rhythmic, as if she had been drugged.

'I wonder if the same thing will happen to them when they get through the door,' Jess said. 'They're just like Madoc, after all.'

'I don't want to hang around to find out,' Carter muttered, 'and I don't see any big exit sign.'

'No,' said Luca, staring at the fireplace. He wondered if they could hide in there but he knew straight away that was ridiculous. It would be the first place Madoc's men would look.

Think. Think. He lifted his head, frustrated. Madoc's men were firing steadily into the door.

'We're running out of time, Luca,' called Carter. 'That wood won't last much longer.'

'We were supposed to come here,' Jess said, 'which means there has to be a way out.'

'It's a shame Peake didn't just tell us,' said Carter, glancing at the doors as they continued to buckle and give.

Luca whirled around, searching up and down for something that might be a clue. The tattered faces of the knights on the banners seemed to mock him. Luca stared into King Arthur's eyes.

'Tell me, damn you!' he shouted in rage. 'Help us!'

The eyes seemed to move a fraction. The faintest ripple passed down the ancient cloth, then another.

'There's a breeze coming from behind the fireplace,' said Jess, already one step ahead of him.

'So?' Carter replied.

'So, there might be a hole in the wall.'

A deafening burst of gunfire sent more splinters flying off the doors. Carter pushed the banner to one side.

'Nothing.'

'It'll be higher,' Jess said.

'Give me a leg up, then. I'll rip the banner down and see.'

'No!' Luca and Jess shouted together.

'Why not?' Carter replied angrily.

'If there's a way out, Madoc's men will spot it as soon as they come in.'

Carter studied her for a moment. Then he smiled.

'You're clever.'

'If you say so. Just don't rip it down.'

They shoved Carter up behind the frayed cloth.

'There's a gap in the wall,' he shouted, 'just big enough to get through. And some kind of light. I can see a tunnel. That's where we need to go.'

He dropped back to the ground, wiping cobwebs from his face and hair.

'I can lift you both up into it,' he said.

'And then you're stuck,' Jess replied. She flinched as the doors cracked and heaved on their hinges.

'No other way. You'll have to wedge yourselves in and lift up Gwen, with me pushing her. After that, pull me up.'

'We can do that,' said Luca.

'I know you can. Ladies first.'

Carter dipped down to let Jess climb onto his shoulders. She eased herself behind the banner.

'It's filthy,' she called out. 'I hate spiders.'

'I hate men with guns,' grunted Carter, swaying left and right.

Jess's feet scrambled against him, then she disappeared.

'Well?' shouted Luca.

'It's narrow, but once you're inside you can turn around. I can see the tunnel. It drops away, so be careful. There's a really bright glow down below. That's what's lighting it up. And there's only room for two of us.'

Carter and Luca exchanged a glance.

'Jess will have to jump down the tunnel. You'll have to pull up Gwen yourself,' Carter said.

Luca had already worked that out. He had no idea if he would be able to.

'I'm coming, Jess,' he said. 'You've got to go.'

'Where to?'

Luca paused.

'Ask me when we get there.'

Jess's face appeared from behind the tapestry.

'Freddie won't be able to follow us.'

'I know.'

She stared at him. He felt completely helpless.

'It's okay, Luca. I know we have to go. Make sure you follow me, yes?'

'Yes.'

She disappeared. Luca waited for her to speak again but there was silence. She had evidently found the courage to jump. He scrambled up, with Carter lifting him as high as he could manage. He turned in the confined space and stared at the distant light.

What the hell is down there? He thought. Suppose I'll find out soon enough.

'Now pull up Gwen.'

Luca struggled to get any kind of grip on her but eventually managed to snag one hand in her hair and the other through her belt. Gwen groaned but she did not wake.

'Go easy, Luca,' Carter said.

'I'm trying to,' he replied, hauling Gwen's dead weight higher. 'This is really hard.'

She slipped back a bit and Luca thought he would lose his grip, but one more enormous effort dragged her through. Luca's shoulder muscles were on fire. He was exhausted, but he had done it. One down, one to go.

'Is she okay?'

'Yeah. I'm going to roll her down the tunnel now.'

'Better get a move on, Luca. I think the doors are gonna break.'

Luca heaved her towards the light. She was either flying through space to somewhere safe or she was about to land in a broken heap, very dead indeed.

'Reach up and grab my hands.'

'Now or never, Luca.'

Luca took hold of Carter's wrists. They were slippery with sweat. He closed his eyes and pulled. Nothing. He pulled again, straining harder.

'Come on,' Carter urged.

Luca breathed slowly.

I can do this, he thought. I can make things happen. A voice whispered to him, very close.

Yes you can, young Pendragon.

'Who's there?' Luca gasped.

I heard you calling me. You said you would help...now I will help you. I can give you the strength to save Lancelot's boy.

'Arthur?'

Yes.

The tapestry pressed against him. The ancient fabric stank of mould and dust. He couldn't push it away because he was holding on to Carter, but suddenly fresh air blew into his lungs and his muscles suddenly surged with energy. He felt as though he could lift a boulder up into the hole.

Now pull.

Luca did so. Carter shot up effortlessly.

'I have no idea how you did that,' he grunted.

'Nor me,' Luca replied. 'Get down that tunnel. If we survive this, I'll tell you what happened.'

Carter took a second to glance down, then he jumped head first towards the light. The doors gave with one last almighty crack. A terrible volley of gunfire exploded through the hall. Luca heard Madoc's men run forwards, calling out as they did so.

'Clear! Clear!'

Luca held his breath. He prepared to jump when he heard Freddie's voice.

'Looks like they've got away,' the boy said.

Silence. Then another voice, calm and chilling.

'Get the kid out of here. And search again. Find them.'

'Good luck with that,' Luca whispered.

He closed his eyes and followed the others down.

***

Madeleine leaned against the cold brickwork of the canteen, staring out into the night. Hug-a-Bug was tucked in her arms, same as it had been since she was old enough to smile. Her breath rose in frosted clouds.

'Four ravens dead,' she murmured. 'Soon be five. You need to hurry up. Ring a ring a roses...ring a ring a roses...'

And above her, in the dark frost tinged sky, Bran circled and called.

27

Luca landed heavily on top of the others. He tried to see where he was but he could only make out white and grey blobs. He heard Jess cry out. Then a hand pushed against his head.

'Get off,' said Carter. 'I can't see anything.'

'Stay calm, you idiot,' Luca shouted as he fended off the flailing arm.

He blinked rapidly, giving his vision time to clear. The whites and greys formed into more solid objects. They were in some kind of yard, with overflowing wheelie bins and piles of sodden cardboard boxes. There were crates of empty bottles stacked against a wall. A jagged hole in the brickwork above them appeared to be the end of the tunnel. The bricks crunched together and the hole was gone. Carter was beside him, rubbing his jaw.

'I think I hit my head on something.'

'Yeah,' grunted Luca. 'Me. Where are we?'

'Not a clue, but I don't think we're still in Camelot. And they can't follow us if the tunnel's gone.'

Gwen was waking up. The wet cardboard had cushioned her fall. She moaned and tried to speak but instead was sick on the floor. Carter found a bottle filled with dirty rain. Gwen slugged it down, swilling the last drops of the murky liquid around her mouth as if it was lemonade.

'We need to get somewhere out of sight,' Carter said, looking around. 'Through there.'

He pointed at a half-open fire door.

'It goes into a restaurant, I think,' Jess said. She scrunched up her eyes, concentrating.

'Freddie feels miles away.'

'Then we're off the island,' Carter replied. 'Come on.'

They lifted Gwen up. As they moved her across the yard, she stiffened. Her eyes widened with terror and she screamed.

'What is it?' Carter asked.

Gwen's hand snaked out. Her finger pointed high, to something behind them. They turned as one, still holding her rigid body.

The Shard loomed over them, its lights piercing the dark clouds above.

***

They moved through the fire door. Gwen was just about able to walk with help.

I'm back at the Shard, she thought, her brain a mess of tumbling images and memories. I tried to get away and I failed. Maybe it's because Camelot knew I'm a Madoc. It didn't want me in there.

The others were tense and silent, eyes fixed on each gloomy corner, each new corridor. Slowly, they made their way to the front of the restaurant. The dirty windows broke up the lights from the glass tower a hundred metres away, casting strange shadows into the room. Gwen collapsed onto a chair.

'What happened to me? I remember walking into that hall, then it really hurt me here.' She touched her chest. 'It's still there, a bit.'

'We got out of Camelot through some kind of tunnel,' said Carter.

'And just ended up in London,' Luca added. 'You know, the kind of stuff that happens to us these days.'

Gwen looked at them. The hunger and fatigue suddenly didn't matter. She felt safe, and something more than that. She didn't feel alone.

Carter moved close and told her everything. When he finished, she leaned over and gave Luca a hug.

'Thank you.'

'I didn't do a lot,' he said. 'Carter was pushing you more than I was pulling. And you saved me when the man was about to shoot. That karate kick stuff was awesome.'

'She's good at that,' Carter interrupted.

'This is all because of my father,' Gwen said. 'I'm so sorry. And now Freddie as well.'

'You're not to blame,' Jess replied. 'You've lost as much as we have. Maybe more.'

A sudden clear vision of her mum shot into Gwen's head. She was swimming in a warm tropical pool on a holiday that felt like a lifetime ago.

'Yes...my mum...she died last year.'

Jess stared at her with a new intensity. A strange shadow passed across the girl's eyes.

'A car crash.'

Gwen swallowed, suddenly feeling sick.

'You saw that?'

'Yeah. Since we put the swords on the table, my head is full of stuff, like Freddie can do. I can do it now as well.'

'We all saw the girl with the red hair,' Carter added. 'Weird, but pretty cool. Anyway, I did it before, didn't I? I knew I had to go to the island and we got there, didn't we, so it's not just Freddie.'

Gwen looked at him, conscious of what he was trying to do.

'You don't need to protect me,' she said, 'even though I'm very grateful. I think what Jess and Luca mean is that we're all here for a reason, whether it's the swords or me because of my father.'

Carter frowned. 'Just trying to help.'

'I know. You are helping. All of you have already helped me more than you'll ever know.'

'I'm really sorry about your mum,' said Luca.

'And you're one of us now,' Jess added.

'Before they came, the men...my father's men...Freddie said I was a murderer.'

She choked back tears. Jess moved in close and wrapped her up in a huge embrace.

'You're not, Gwen. And Freddie didn't mean it. He's young and angry, but he's a good kid.'

'Well, maybe I can explain it all to him soon, when we find him,' Gwen whispered. Because we will, Jess. I promise.'

153

'I know we will,' Jess replied.

'One way or the other,' continued Gwen, 'you all saved me. You...you're the best friends I've ever had.' She looked down. 'I don't deserve you.'

'Forget it,' Luca said. 'That promise you just made...same here.'

Gwen glanced through the windows at the blazing lights of the Shard.

'I can make this right,' she said. 'I know what I've got to do.'

***

Gabriel scrambled up the cliff, his fingers raw and bleeding. One by one, the men followed him. Their prisoner's eyes glared like those of a wild dog. Gabriel punched a button on his phone. Randall answered immediately.

'Well?'

'We found the underground place. A castle, by a lake. All kinds of crazy, Randall.'

'And the children?'

'Gwendoline escaped. I don't know how she did it. We got one of the kids, that's all. And the old man you said would be there...he's dead. Kind of.'

Hissing static. No words.

'You still there, Randall?'

'Mr Madoc won't be pleased, Gabriel.'

'You think I don't know that? He'll understand when I tell him what we saw here. This place gives me the creeps.'

'Save your excuses. What do you need?'

Gabriel looked around at his bedraggled team.

'A helicopter to get us off this island.'

'That will take a while to organise. You're on your own until then.'

The phone went dead. Gabriel cursed at it then issued orders to his men.

'You're scared,' said the boy.

Gabriel jumped.

'What did you say?'

'You heard me. Who are you scared of? Is it Madoc?'

'Shut up before I do it for you.'

Gabriel turned away, busying himself with his kit. Freddie shrugged and looked out over the choppy sea. On the horizon, visible only if you knew where to look, a thin black cloud seemed to be heading for the mainland.

***

In his office, high above London, Madoc stood motionless beneath the suspended table. He glanced at the screen of his tablet. The fifth light turned red. The sixth was amber. Just one green light remained.

28

Two days had passed - eating scraps, little sleep and shivering in the dark. Luca stared out of the window and sniffed.

Just a cold, he told himself. A normal, miserable cold. At least it won't kill me.

The few working street lights cast a watery yellow glow onto the deserted street. The Shard was lit up like a cheerful department store at Christmas, but it looked more like a giant tombstone. He wiped his hands across his face.

I need a shower, he thought. Not much chance of that any time soon.

Carter shuffled up beside him.

'Couldn't sleep?'

'No,' Luca said.

'Same here. Any sign of life?'

'Just the usual switch over.'

'Every eight hours, just like clockwork.'

'Yeah. Wonder where they go?'

Carter shrugged.

'To visit their nan, for all I know. Or just going out looking for people to kill. Anyway, it doesn't matter. It gives us a way in when the doors open.'

Luca didn't answer. He wasn't sure he had the strength for another argument. All he wanted to do was get to the Tower and find the girl. The sword was doing something to him, making him think differently, allowing him to hear sounds that he would have once ignored. The girl was real. She was calling him even more loudly now that he was so close.

'Well?' Carter asked, breaking into his thoughts.

'I can't stop thinking about when I pulled you up. That was *the* King Arthur I heard.'

'I don't care if it was the tooth fairy. I wouldn't be here otherwise.'

'Carter, whatever happens, promise me one thing.'

'Go on.'

'You'll come back to Lundy with me. And bring Gwen with you.'

'No chance. Remember what happened to her last time?'

'Exactly. We've got unfinished business. I want her to go in there as one of us, not as a Madoc.'

Carter was silent for a few moments.

'That's a big promise, mate.'

'Think about it, yeah?'

'Yeah. Now your turn. Agree to what Gwen wants.'

'It's a lunatic idea. Anyway, we could be at the Tower in thirty minutes. Maybe save the ravens, stop all this somehow.'

He knew what Carter's reply would be, even as he spoke.

'No. We've been over this.'

Luca sighed. The others were winning the argument.

'But the girl with the red hair...'

'What about her? Has she got the vaccine? Can *she* make them better? Or Jess's kid brother...your mum?'

Luca glared out of the window. What else could he say, because deep down, he knew Carter was right.

'I can't help what's in my head. A bit like you, when you came to us.'

'Fair enough. But this is different. We've got the swords all charged up. We can do something amazing first before we go there. And you promised Jess...'

'I know what I promised.'

Carter moved so that he was in Luca's line of sight.

'If you rescue the kid, I reckon Jess will love you forever.'

Luca blushed. Was it that obvious how he felt about her? He quickly changed the subject.

'We'll never get in. There might be thousands of guards in there.'

'Hundreds, actually.'

He turned. Gwen had joined them. She looked exhausted. There were dark rings under her eyes and her hair was dull with dirt.

'And I don't really care how many, to be honest,' she said. 'I'm going back into the Shard and I'm not leaving without Freddie and the vaccines.'

'Really?' Luca replied. 'And we just walk up to the front door and ask for some? It's not going to happen.'

'Then why are we here?' asked Carter. 'That tunnel just happened to drop us right by the Shard for no reason? And what was the point of me finding Gwen?

158

And all the stuff you lot went through before we even got there? You're wrong, Luca. We're special. We can save people. We can save our families.'

It was a powerful argument. Luca struggled to reply.

'And Freddie's in there,' continued Carter, 'Gwen's ready to rescue him. That's her choice.'

Luca glanced at Gwen. Her face was set hard, her head cocked at just enough of an angle to let him know exactly what she wanted.

'In eight hours,' she said, 'when the vans switch over again, we need to move.'

They fell silent again, staring at the immense bulk of the Shard. Luca wished Peake was there, and he missed Bran's pecks and squawks. He hoped the clever old bird was safe somewhere.

'Freddie's definitely in there, isn't he?' he asked Carter. 'I mean, if we go in and he's not...'

'If Jess says he's in there, he's in there.'

'He is.'

Luca jumped. Jess was beside him, moving on silent feet. She looked like a ghost. Her arms were crossed and her hair hung around her face, but her eyes hadn't lost any of their colour. Luca didn't think he had ever seen anyone look more beautiful.

'My brother gave us a chance. Now we go and get him. Luca, you promised.'

'I did. But the girl, Jess. It's like a...like an itch or something. It's there all the time.'

'The Shard first, then we go to the Tower.'

'I could go by myself.'

'Don't be stupid,' Carter said. 'We won't let you.'

'Carter's right,' added Jess. 'The bit about us not letting you, that is.'

Luca balled his fists. He breathed hard, fighting back the anger, but he knew it was no good. They were going in whether he liked it or not. It felt like suicide.

'It's why we're here,' Gwen said.

'And you know,' interrupted Carter, 'whatever happens, I wouldn't have missed all this.'

Luca looked at each of them, and at that moment he felt exactly the same.

'Okay,' he said. 'At the next switch over, we do it.'

'At last,' Carter replied, punching the air.

***

Behind the smoked glass windows of the Shard's foyer, Randall looked through his night vision binoculars. He could see figures moving in the shadows of the smashed up restaurant. Two nights, now. They would have to make their move soon.

'Ready when you are, kids,' he whispered.

29

The plan was so simple it might just work. They had discovered an alley that came out near the Shard. It meant they could approach without being seen. Then there was the next part, which Luca tried to pretend was inspired when in fact it sounded more crazy with each telling.

Every eight hours, a metal roller door opened as a fleet of vans cruised up to it. Others then left the Shard. When the vans passed each other, they were going to duck behind and use them as a shield. That way, they could slide beneath the roller door before it came down. After that...well, there wasn't much point asking questions because nobody had an answer.

A simple plan. And almost definitely hopeless.

They left without a backward glance. Luca's mouth was dry but there was no more time for worrying. At the end of the alley he leaned forwards to check the street then quickly dived back.

'Damn.'

A large group of people was moving towards them.

'I don't believe this,' Carter said. 'Who the hell are they?'

'Most of them look ill,' said Jess. 'There's some really young kids with them, see?'

Luca counted around thirty men, women and children. Some were walking reasonably well, others were dragging themselves along in obvious pain. Their faces were a horrible pale yellow in the glow of the lights. He could see the blood in their eyes. He remembered his mum and the sudden memory was like a punch in the gut. This wasn't a game. This was real, with millions of lives at stake.

One of the youngest children was crying. He looked no older than five. A woman was holding the boy's hand but her expression was vacant. The child coughed fresh blood down the front of his filthy coat.

'Keep back,' said Carter. 'They might attack us if they see us.'

'They're getting closer,' Gwen whispered. Luca heard the tension in her voice. He felt it too. The mob was already half-dead, with nothing to lose. A few more corpses wouldn't matter much either way. Luca made a decision.

'Go,' he urged the others.

'Too early,' argued Carter. 'The vans won't be here for another twenty minutes.'

'Tough. Run!'

They dashed across the street and just managed to squeeze in behind an abandoned car. Carter lay down and sneaked a look.

'We weren't seen. They're only interested in the doors of the Shard.'

Luca did the same as Carter, lying flat on his belly so that he could peer out from under the car. He watched the first brick thrown by the crowd, then the next. They bounced harmlessly off the Shard's reinforced glass. The people started to shout, demanding food and medicine.

At that moment, the roller door began to grind open. A solitary van crawled out into the street. Four armed men followed, dressed in black combats like their attackers at Camelot. They carried the same weapons and they looked ready to use them.

'Fan out,' the lead man shouted, running forwards.

Luca held his breath but the men didn't look their way. They were focused on the brick throwers. The van led the way, moving more quickly now. The men took up positions on either side of the vehicle. The crowd noticed them for the first time. It didn't look like food and medicine was forthcoming.

'This is our chance,' urged Carter, tugging at Luca's arm. 'Let's get in, quick!'

Luca couldn't tear his eyes away from the child with the blood stained coat. His voice suddenly cut across the empty space.

'Have they come to make us better, mummy?'

Luca wanted to run to the boy and scoop him up but he was frozen to the spot.

'Now, Luca. Get a move on!'

One by one, they scuttled through into the dark tunnel just as the gunfire started.

'We've got to help them,' Luca said, fighting back at Carter.

'And all get killed as well? Don't be stupid. They were dead already.'

And Luca understood there was nothing that Madoc wouldn't do.

Nothing at all.

30

The tunnel was about fifty metres long, sloping gently downwards. Fluorescent lights flickered and buzzed overhead. No alarms sounded as the children ran, their footsteps echoing loudly on the concrete floor. There were more open doors at the far end of the tunnel, revealing a brightly lit car park.

'We can't stay here,' Luca said. 'They'll be back in once they've finished what they're doing. Gwen, which way?'

'Straight down there.'

'Okay.' Luca paused. 'You all right?'

Gwen nodded.

'Those people were innocent,' she said. 'If any of you didn't already know why we're here, you do now.'

There was nothing the others could say in reply. Outside, the gunfire grew more sporadic then died away completely. The work was done, it seemed.

'Will there be any guards?' Luca asked.

'There's always a man in a little room,' Gwen replied. 'He used to wave at me when we drove past.'

'Let's hope he doesn't get a chance to wave at you now.'

Luca edged closer to the doors. Light spilled through onto the floor of the tunnel. He listened but could hear nothing from inside.

'In we go.'

The car park was cavernous and full of vehicles. There were dozens of black vans, twenty of the Range Rovers and a row of expensive looking motorbikes. Carter whistled softly at those.

'Ducati Streetfighters. Nice bits of kit.'

'My dad likes to ride them,' Gwen said. 'And he likes to win.'

She pointed towards the far corner.

'That's where the security guard's room is, and the lifts.'

'So where will Freddie be?'

'I'm guessing he's been taken to the top where Randall can keep an eye on him.'

'I don't like the sound of Randall.'

'He's bad news, Luca. Remember what I told you about him. He knows everything.'

Before he could answer, Luca heard the sound of the van entering the tunnel. They ducked down behind the nearest vehicle. The van's engine noise echoed loudly as the men walked into the car park. They were silent, their guns held loosely by their sides. Their gloves were smeared with blood.

'They can stay in there for now,' said one of the men, apparently in charge. 'Dump them in the river tomorrow, okay?'

The two men nodded. They stripped off their gloves and opened the back of the van to throw them in. Jess's gasp was stifled quickly by Gwen's hand across her mouth. It was full of bodies.

The men slammed the doors shut and walked over to the guard's room. The leader tapped on the glass. A burly man in a dark green jacket sat up, headphones tumbling from his ears. He looked surprised, then scared.

'Asleep again, Fletcher? We were only gone five minutes. I've told you before, you can easily go and join the party outside if you don't pull your weight.'

'No, Gabriel,' the guard stammered. 'Just checking a few things. Knew you were there. Honest, I did.'

Fletcher kept up the steady stream of excuses until he was lifted off his feet and slammed against a wall.

'Shut it. Next time, I tell Randall.'

Fletcher's mouth flapped but he didn't speak. Gabriel dropped him down, bored.

'Get out of my way.'

Fletcher rubbed at his throat, panting.

'I heard you saw a man change into a bear. Is that right?'

Gabriel paused.

'You talk too much. Just do your job, okay? Get the main doors closed.'

'What about the vaccines? Are they still going out tonight?'

'No. Delivery's cancelled. Randall's orders.'

Fletcher nodded eagerly, desperate to please. Gabriel ignored him and led his team out of the car park through the stairwell door. The door clanged shut and

Fletcher visibly jumped. Then he dusted himself down and went back into his room, muttering loudly.

'So now we know what the vans have been doing. And there won't be anybody else down here tonight,' whispered Carter. 'We just need to get past the guard.'

He grabbed a fire extinguisher.

'Luca, get his attention. When he comes out, I'll smack him with this. Time to start fighting back, eh?'

The plan worked perfectly. Luca shimmied his way across to the office, rapped on the window and gave Fletcher a big smile. The stunned guard opened the door just as Carter brought the extinguisher crashing down on the back of his head.

Fletcher hit the floor with a loud groan.

'Get his belt off and strap his ankles together,' said Carter. 'Use his shoe laces to tie his wrists to the chair. He won't go anywhere in a hurry.'

Fletcher's face was grey and his eyes didn't seem to be focusing.

'So, boss,' said Carter, turning to Luca, 'you're in charge. What next?'

Luca's mind was clear and focused, any trace of doubt washed away by the terrible sight of the bodies in the van.

'Jess needs to be there when Freddie's found,' said Luca. 'I'll go with her. You and Gwen look for the vaccine. Once you've found it, grab as much as you can and meet us back here. You've got two hours. If we don't show up, get to the Tower.'

'We won't leave without you.'

'See you in two hours, then?'

'Don't be late,' replied Carter.

Carter held out a hand to shake. Luca remembered how he had done the same and how Carter had refused. And before that, he had ignored Peake's hand in the lighthouse.

'Good luck,' he said, gripping Carter's hand.

The lift door opened and Luca led them into the heart of the Shard.

***

Randall was alone in the control room. He had dismissed the security staff and locked the door. Only he could see the images on the bank of CCTV cameras that flickered in front of him. One showed the outside of the Shard, where a few minutes earlier the crowd had gathered. More people had arrived, attracted by the gunfire. They held back, obviously shocked by the blood-soaked pavements.

He looked at another screen that was dark and grainy, with a fish-eye view of the car park. Randall leaned in closely. He smiled. The camera was too small and well-hidden to be spotted by the children.

'Welcome to the Shard,' he said.

Then he stood up and left the room, his pistol already drawn.

31

They made their way along a dark corridor. Luca hardly dared breathe as he padded along the thick carpet. He didn't know if he was succeeding in looking calm. He didn't want Jess to think he was utterly terrified, but he guessed his thoughts were booming out anyway. The walls were covered with enormous prints of Madoc News exclusives, reproductions of front pages and grinning mug shots of their most famous newsreaders from across the globe. Every pair of eyes seemed to follow him.

'What do you reckon, Jess?' he whispered.

'We're getting nearer to him.'

She frowned.

'What is it?' Luca asked.

'I don't know. It's like he's trying to reach me but at the same time, he's telling me to get away.'

They continued on. Luca felt a growing sense of foreboding. They halted next to a large smoked glass door with a large red *M* stencilled across it.

'This is it,' Jess said. 'Freddie's in there, but something's wrong. This has been too easy.'

The door opened. Two armed guards leaped out.

'Don't move!' shouted one.

A moment later, a man in a dark suit stepped into the corridor.

'Hello,' he said, his face wreathed in a smile.

Luca instantly recognised John Madoc. His dark eyes were like those of a wolf, unblinking and completely without fear. An ugly lead gargoyle hung around his neck.

'I didn't see this,' Jess said.

'No, young lady,' Madoc replied. 'I made sure your special talents were useless here.'

He touched the gargoyle. 'This blocks your silly mind games. Did you know that such a thing existed?'

Jess looked utterly distraught.

'Peake had one the same.'

Madoc laughed out loud.

'So that's what the old fool called himself. And he obviously didn't want you poking around in his head.' He smiled, like a fox about to bite a rabbit. 'Wonder what he was ashamed of? Well, don't just stand there. Please come into my office and join my other guest.'

***

'This has to be where the production lines are. I heard my father talking to Randall about it.'

Gwen and Carter approached a dimly lit laboratory.

'Can we just go in?'

'I don't know. I kind of thought it would be busy.'

'Well, good that it isn't. Come on,' Carter urged as he pushed the door.

Gwen waited for alarms to blare out but nothing happened. She followed him in. They worked quickly, checking every cupboard and drawer. The minutes ticked by.

'There's nothing here, Carter. No vaccines.'

'There's another door over there.'

Gwen peered through. Long steel rollers ran from one end to the other, and she saw what appeared to be massive refrigerators along one wall.

'That could be it,' she whispered.

They crept in, hardly daring to breathe. Carter opened one of the fridges. He whistled softly.

'Bingo.'

Dozens of polystyrene boxes were stacked inside. Gwen took one out and lifted the lid. The box was full of syringes.

'I had a single injection. There must be thousands in here.' A thought struck her. 'Maybe you should have one.'

'What? Stick a needle in myself? No thanks. I reckon I'm okay, Gwen.'

'Well, grab a box each and let's get out of here. I can't believe it's been this easy.'

As she finished speaking the lights blinked out, leaving them in total darkness.

'Carter!' Gwen hissed. 'What happened?'

She dropped the box and groped at thin air, panicked.

'I didn't touch anything,' he said.

Someone was in there with them. Gwen instinctively ducked down, ready to strike in self-defence. Torchlight exploded in her face. She swerved and kicked out. Her foot connected but it was only a glancing blow. She rolled forwards and her hands chopped down, hoping to land a better hit but the newcomer was too quick.

Gwen kicked out and slipped on the polished floor. She was off balance and falling, then her feet were swept away from under her.

'Be careful,' a deep voice boomed. 'Somebody could get hurt.'

The lights buzzed back on. Gwen looked up, knowing exactly who she was going to see.

'Good evening, Gwendoline,' Randall said. His pistol was pointed directly at Carter, sprawled helplessly on the floor next to Gwen. 'And to you, young man. My name is Randall.'

He picked up the box.

'The vaccines. Two hundred doses. More than enough for all the laboratories in Britain to start making their own.'

Carter tried to try and grab it. Gwen spread her arm across in front of him.

'Don't,' she said. 'If he shoots he won't miss.'

'Thank you, Gwendoline,' said Randall. 'I have no desire to shoot anybody. And you nearly got me with that last kick, but not quite. Now please stand up, both of you.'

They did as they were told. Gwen slipped her hand into Carter's. She wanted Randall to see that they weren't scared and she wanted him to know that they were united.

'Your father has been waiting to see you. We won't keep him waiting much longer.' Randall instructed them both to sit down. 'First, we need to have a little chat.'

32

Madoc's guards dragged Luca roughly to a chair and tied his arms to it. The knots bit into his skin, but he made sure he didn't let on how painful it was. Jess was bundled next to her brother. Madoc stared at their swords like a starving man at a feast.

'Leave us,' he instructed his men.

Once the door was closed, Madoc grinned.

'Time for the formal introductions. I'm sure you already know *my* name. Freddie and I are acquainted, of course. He's very brave for one so young, but Randall, my head of security, was able to extract quite a lot of information. You'll meet him soon and I should point out that he's not a very nice man.'

Madoc chuckled at his own joke.

'Your plan wasn't the most sophisticated thing, was it? I would have hoped for something more eye-catching from that old fraud Merlin, or Peake, or whatever he wants to call himself, but now he's dead, who cares?'

Luca looked down, horrified. Madoc seemed to know everything.

'Oh dear,' Madoc purred at him. 'You look so disappointed. Do you still expect him to come flying in through a window and save you?'

Madoc walked along the back of the chairs.

'You're Freddie's sister, of course,' he said as he passed Jess. 'The family resemblance is obvious. And you, young man, must think yourself very important. I've tracked you with interest since Peake did his party trick in Winchester. What's your name?'

Luca swallowed hard. He glanced at Freddie. He looked ready to fight with everything he had. Luca decided to do the same.

'My name's Lucan Pendragon Broom,' he croaked.

He cleared his throat, desperate to hear his voice sound stronger.

'We're here to rescue Freddie. We're going to stop you, you murderer.'

Madoc threw back his head and roared with laughter.

'Please, tell me more. I love a good joke.'

Madoc shoved his face into Luca's. His hot breath was minty. His eyes were like slits.

'You think *you're* the Pendragon? You think you can beat me? Peake probably said you were special. He was wrong - you're nothing. Now look at this.'

Madoc held up a tablet.

'One light for each of the ravens at the Tower. Did your magical friend bother to explain the importance of them? My computer systems are hacked into their microchips. As a bird dies a light changes from green to red. As you can see, we're counting down to the final raven.'

Madoc flicked the tablet. The fireplace died and the wall spun around. He walked underneath the massive round table and held up a book. The cover appeared to be made of wood, with pages of wrinkled skin.

I hope that's not human, Luca thought with a shiver. He stared at the painted face of Madoc as king.

'Nice table,' he said, trying to sound brave. 'Not the real one, though.'

'Real?' spat Madoc. 'What do you know? Time for a history lesson, boy. Peake wrote this book of spells thousands of years ago but he lost it at the battle of Bosworth when Richard the last Plantagenet king was slaughtered by the stupid Tudors. My ancestor managed to grab the book and it's been hidden ever since. That should have been the end of Peake's interfering but he always comes back, time and time again.'

Madoc flashed a feline smile.

'By the look on your face, Master Broom, it doesn't appear he was that forthcoming with the truth,' said Madoc. 'Did he explain that the ravens can't be killed by men? They have to die of disease. And he clearly never told you that *he* wrote the spell that's making all this happen, to remove any king if they became too powerful. That's right, *Pendragon*. Your precious Peake made the plague and he's why the ravens are dying. And now I'm going to use his own magic against you all.'

***

The three children sat in silence. Madoc prowled around the room, pleased with himself and with good reason - he was in complete control. Luca tried to catch Jess's attention but she and Freddie were focused only on each other.

Suddenly, Jess's head nodded, the tiniest of movements but enough for Luca to see. Freddie's eyes switched to Luca and locked onto him. It was a deeply unsettling feeling, like being examined through the bars of a cage.

Freddie smiled. Just then, the electronic door lock buzzed quietly.

'More guests,' Madoc said.

The door opened and Luca's heart sank. It was Gwen and Carter, followed by a fierce looking man in a dark suit. A red letter M tie pin glittered in the lights. The man held a pistol and a rucksack.

'I found these two in the laboratory,' said the man. 'They were looking for the vaccines.'

Madoc stared at Gwen. She stared back, her face cold and emotionless.

'Well done, Randall,' whispered Madoc.

The door clicked shut. Madoc turned his attention to Carter.

'So you're the boy we saw in the video.'

Madoc examined Carter's sword.

'Lancelot's,' he said.

Carter held Madoc's gaze, not backing down.

You're braver than me, Luca thought. I nearly wet myself when I first saw him.

But Carter was scared - there was the slightest tremble in his hands as Madoc spoke again.

'Let me enlighten you. My men managed to film you just before they were murdered by that mob. We've tracked you using the GPS installed in Gwendoline's watch. You led me to Camelot and you brought my daughter home. I'm very grateful.'

Carter's head dropped.

'Don't take it too badly, boy. Did you really think a nobody like you could beat me?'

'You tracked me without my knowledge for years,' Gwendoline hissed.

'Yes,' her father said. 'Clearly it was the right thing to do based on your recent behaviour.'

'I left here because of you and I went with Carter because I wanted to, you monster. We know all about your plan. We know you released the virus. And I know I hate you.'

She unclasped the watch and hurled it at her father. It bounced off his chest and clattered onto the floor.

Madoc seemed to be searching for the right words.

'Given time, you'll understand I had no choice. This is my destiny and yours too. All I've ever done is try to keep you safe. I've provided you with everything you ever wanted. I know it's not been easy for you since your mother died, but...'

'Don't you dare talk about her,' said Gwen, cutting through him. 'For all I know, you killed her too.'

Madoc's face darkened. Luca didn't think they had long to live.

'That's enough, young lady. I'll forgive you that comment just as I'm willing to forgive your betrayal of me. I imagine you've been told all sorts of lies. Well, we can put it behind us, you and me. Once we're finished here we'll talk it all through.'

Gwen glowered at him.

'I'd rather die than spend another second anywhere near you.'

Then she raised herself up to her tallest height and spat in her father's face.

Madoc closed his eyes for a moment, then they flashed open. Luca wouldn't have believed a human could look so much like a snake if he hadn't seen it himself.

'So be it,' Madoc said. 'A shame. I see you're one of them now. And yes, I'm afraid your suspicions were right. I did have your mother killed. She was the same as you, always looking for the good in people. She didn't agree with my methods. She didn't believe in the power of the Madoc name. So she had to die.'

Gwen crouched, ready to attack. Then she sagged at the knees, the will to fight gone. Carter slipped a hand under each armpit and she fell back against him.

'Very touching,' snarled Madoc, 'Carter, is it? Just what I would expect from the foul offspring of Lancelot. Always the charmer, always ready to catch a girl's eye. I think you've just volunteered to die first, boy.'

Madoc turned to Randall.

'I'm bored of this. Are there any more of these vermin polluting my building?'

'No, sir. The searches haven't found any more trespassers.'

'Good. Dispose of them. And you should all understand I'll soon be in charge of an emergency government of top scientists, expert doctors, leaders in their field. Every one of them is completely loyal to me. When the final raven is cold in its box, Britain will be mine.'

'And that, Mr Madoc, is where you're wrong.'

Randall levelled his pistol directly at Madoc's head. He touched a control panel on the wall. A thick steel shutter dropped down over the door and windows. Then he reached inside his shirt and pulled out a gold sword.

33

'What are you doing, Randall?' Madoc asked.

Luca was thinking exactly the same thing. Then he noticed that Jess and Freddie were smiling and nodding. And then most surprising of all, Carter slapped Randall on the back.

'I wasn't sure you were going to go through with it,' he said.

Nothing made sense. Madoc's mouth was open. His arms were by his side. His face had taken on a deathly pale hue and he was shaking slightly.

'Randall, if this is supposed to be some kind of joke, I'm not laughing.'

'No joke,' Randall said. 'You're not in charge here any more, Mr Madoc. We are. Carter, untie your friends.'

Carter worked swiftly. He freed Jess and Freddie, then moved across to Luca.

'What's going on?' Luca asked.

'You'll find out in a minute.' Carter pointed at Madoc. 'Oh, the look on your face, mate. Priceless.'

'Randall, extend me the courtesy of an explanation. That is, before you're permanently relieved of your position and your life.'

'Anger and bravado,' Randall replied. 'Just what I expected from you. Sit down.'

Randall waved the gun towards one of the recently occupied chairs but Madoc didn't move.

'I don't take orders, Randall. I give them.'

'Your choice. I don't really care whether you sit or stand to hear what I've got to say. You employed me as a loyal bodyguard who would do whatever you ordered regardless of how unpleasant or evil it was. Well, we've certainly done our fair share of evil things.'

Madoc didn't flinch. He didn't even blink, but his face had grown pale.

'You look shocked. Good. That means you've genuinely never suspected my secret. The Plantagenet kings knew that the Madocs wanted revenge. My family was chosen to track yours over the years, watching for when the mad lust for power rose again. And it was obvious from an early age that you were the maddest of them all.'

'You treacherous worm,' growled Madoc. 'I gave you everything and this is how you repay me.'

'You've given me nothing except guilt and regret. I've done terrible things for you to protect my true identity. I'll have to live with that.'

'Spare me the pitiful speech. And who's here to help you now? Peake's gone. He's not coming back. Gabriel saw him drown.' Madoc spat out the words, his eyes blazing. 'You won't get five metres outside of this room.'

'Really?' Randall replied. 'I devised every security device in this building. We're all going to walk out of here, taking the vaccines with us. They'll be delivered to the government within the hour. And you will spend the rest of your life in prison.'

Madoc laughed unpleasantly.

'And you think they'll let you off with a slap on the wrist? Not a chance. You'll be in the cell next to me, Randall. I'll scream at you day and night until you go insane.'

'That's the price I agreed to pay when I knew I had to do this. My freedom is a small sacrifice to make.'

'You're forgetting the ravens and the spell, you fool. Nothing can stop that. Britain will fall and I will be the next Pendragon, the true monarch.'

'Shut up, you lunatic,' Randall snapped.

He took a roll of thick tape from his pocket and stuck a strip roughly across Madoc's mouth. Then he taped his wrists together after relieving him of the book. As Madoc wriggled, there was a flash of gold at his neck. Carter jumped forwards.

'Hey, look at this,' he shouted, reaching into Madoc's shirt. He held up the black diamond sword. 'He's got one as well.'

They crowded round to look. The eyes of the skull glittered.

'It feels evil,' said Jess, 'like it was made by a...'

She seemed to search for the right word. Freddie touched her forehead.

'I think it was made by a witch,' he said. 'I can almost hear her laughing. Don't like it.'

'Horrible thing,' Jess shuddered.

'So what do we do with it?' Carter asked. He paused. 'Mr Randall, is it Gwen's?'

Luca looked at Gwen. For a moment, her eyes focused on the sword. The diamond gleamed in the light. Gwen reached out, then pulled her hand away.

'I...I don't want it anywhere near me.'

'I'll look after it,' Randall said. 'I don't think any of you kids should touch it. And thanks for trusting me in the laboratory. I know it was a big thing to ask.'

'Who are you, Randall?' Luca asked. He struggled to hold back his anger. 'You're supposed to be Madoc's mate and now you're ours?'

'My ancestor was Sir Bedivere, one of the original knights. Many years ago, a sword was brought by a raven to my great-great-great grandfather's house. The bird was able to talk to him somehow, or so the story goes. He told my relative about our family, and that he had a job to do. He had to track down a man called Madoc and from then on, be ready to act. So the Randalls have done exactly that. I've spent years getting close to Gwen's father, gaining his trust, working from the inside. It's been horrible and dangerous, but I had no choice. And that raven's always been there, watching over me. He's called Bran.'

'Bloody hell!' Carter laughed. 'That bird has been around forever.'

Luca smiled in spite of his rage. He would have given anything for Bran to be there now, pecking at his fingers.

'We know Bran,' he said. 'He helped us escape Madoc's men. You know, the ones who were trying to kill us.'

'I understand your anger and I can't ever explain just how relieved I am that you're all okay. Freddie told me your mum's ill. I'm so sorry.'

'Sorry?' replied Luca. 'Sorry doesn't quite do it. My mum's probably dead because of what you and Madoc have done!'

He couldn't stop himself. He dived forwards, ready to rip this man's eyes out. Randall swerved to one side. Luca was attacking fresh air. Then his arm was bent up his back.

'Don't fight me, Luca. I can kill you in an instant. Please listen to what I have to say.'

Luca struggled away from Randall and he lunged again, all of the pent-up anger and tiredness of the last few days coming together. His fists flailed against nothing as Randall easily side stepped him. Luca collapsed, sobbing.

'You could have stopped all this. You could have.'

'No, mate,' said Carter. 'He told us everything. Madoc found the plague buried in an old box right under where we are now, sealed away to stop it spreading. He knew where to look because the location was written in Peake's book. Randall didn't think that

Madoc would ever find it but he hired someone to translate the old languages. And Gwen's mum...'

'...was killed,' Gwen interrupted. There was no emotion in her voice but her eyes gleamed with passion as she crouched in front of Luca.

'Yes,' said Randall. 'It was Gabriel. He sabotaged the car, on her father's orders, because she was going to leave and take Gwen with her. She never stood a chance.'

Luca looked at her, searching for any sign this was a trick.

'Are you completely sure we can trust him?'

Gwen nodded.

'I'm so sorry,' repeated Randall. 'I would have stopped him but he released the plague without me knowing. I thought he was going to use it as threat, not as an actual weapon. That was when I acted. The woman who saved Gwen and Carter was my agent. I haven't heard from her since and I doubt she's still alive. And if you had all been captured you'd be here now anyway, which is where you needed to be.'

'It's a miracle none of us have been killed,' said Luca, anger still burning. 'Freddie was kidnapped and Peake's dead. Couldn't you have just chucked Madoc off the roof, or something?'

'I didn't have any choice,' Randall said. 'There was no way of finding out who you were or where Camelot was. Merlin...Peake, you say he's called...has never contacted me or helped me. It was just something my family kept secret – stay under cover, stay close to the Madocs, and act when necessary. You see, Luca, I'm a child of Camelot, too.'

'So you've just been working alone all these years, waiting for when Madoc goes crazy?'

'That's about the top and bottom of it, yes.'

'Mr Randall explained who he was when I arrived,' Freddie said. 'We pretended he was questioning me to keep Madoc happy. He said we should just wait for you all and here you are. We're all back together.'

A sudden piercing alarm sounded and flashing lights went off. The room dimmed to a red glow.

'What's that?' asked Luca.

'I don't know,' Randall replied. 'I designed all the alarms in the building and that's not one I recognise. Unless...'

He pushed Madoc over and roughly searched him.

'I could find out if I can read his mind,' Freddie said.

He ripped off the lead gargoyle, ignoring the man's struggles. He touched Madoc's forehead, grimaced and shivered, suddenly flushed and sweating.

'You okay, Freddie?'

Luca sat down next to him. Freddie didn't look so good.

'Yeah. I don't want to be in his head again. There's a hidden alarm built into his ring. He pressed it just now.'

'Oh, no,' said Randall, spinning Madoc around to see. 'He must have installed it without me knowing. The guards will be alerted.'

In spite of the situation, Randall laughed.
'So he didn't really trust me, after all.'

34

Randall tried the door into his office. It wouldn't budge.

'Damn,' he said. 'The alarm has locked it down. We're trapped in here.'

Randall's eyes narrowed, deep in thought.

'What is it with us lot and doors?' Carter said. 'Luca, can't we do the sword thing again? Smash it open, somehow?'

'I don't know how they work any more than you do.'

'We could just go over the top.'

They all turned to look at Freddie, still sat on the floor. He wiped the sweat off his face and pointed at the ceiling.

'You've got a gun, Randall. Blow a hole in the ceiling and I'll crawl through the air conditioning. Simple.'

Randall grinned.

'How old are you?'

'People always ask me that,' Freddie said.

'I'm not surprised,' Randall replied.

He lifted Madoc's chin.

'This is for all the innocents you've killed,' he said, then thumped Madoc hard. He squirmed and groaned but Randall hit him again. 'That's for the ones we won't be able to save.'

Randall delivered another blow to the temple. Madoc dropped like a brick, unconscious.

'And that was for Gwen's mum. Because she didn't deserve to die. Now stand back. Put your fingers in your ears.'

He pointed his pistol upwards and pulled the trigger four times. The noise was shocking. The room filled with smoke and half of the ceiling crashed down. Once the dust had settled they could see the bullets had torn away enough to reveal a pipe about a metre in diameter with a square access hatch. There was fresh banging on the steel shutters.

'Fast as you can, Freddie,' Luca said. 'We've got visitors.'

Freddie rose to his feet. Randall hoisted him up onto his shoulders. Freddie grabbed the pipe and unclipped the hatch. He climbed through and was gone. They could hear him shuffling along.

'He needs to hurry,' Randall said, one eye on the shutters. A new noise had started. 'They've brought up ox-acetylene torches to burn through.'

Even as Randall spoke, Luca noticed smoke. He didn't think he was imagining the temperature rising in the room, either.

'How long?'

Randall shrugged.

'A few minutes, probably.'

'Just like the great hall again,' Carter groaned. 'I'm really starting to hate doors.'

Then two things happened. The shutter began to melt into a molten blob. At the same moment the door to Randall's office clicked open.

Freddie was covered in plaster dust and there were fresh scratches on his face and knuckles. He was limping slightly but he seemed to be relatively unharmed.

'Well done, mate,' said Luca. 'You've just saved all of our lives.'

'I know,' Freddie replied. 'Now let's get out of here.'

Randall heaved Madoc upright. Luca grabbed the book and ran after the others. The door locked behind him just as the first bullets slammed into it.

***

Randall's office was an enormous circular room, empty except for a desk, a chair and a lift door. Twenty screens ran along one wall in a long horizontal block and every one was tuned into the same scene of an angry crowd jostling with soldiers outside Downing Street.

...BREAKING NEWS...PARLIAMENT DISSOLVED TOMORROW...JOHN MADOC TO LEAD EMERGENCY ADMINISTRATION...BREAKING NEWS...

'The world's gone mad,' said Randall.

'Are we too late?'

'No, Luca. If we can get the vaccines out of here, we can expose Madoc for what he is.'

'What about the ravens?'

'I hoped you'd have an answer to that.'

'We just know we've got to save them,' Luca replied. 'At least Peake bothered to tell us that bit. There's somebody at the Tower who can help us.'

'Do you know who it is?'

'No. Sorry.'

He dropped his eyes, embarrassed.

'So we worry about that when we get there,' said Randall.

He pressed his thumb against a tiny glass screen next to the lift.

'Fingerprint lock. They won't be able to follow us. Get in, all of you.'

There were only two buttons, one for up and one for down. Randall pressed the latter and they dropped rapidly. Luca swallowed hard to clear his ears and his stomach.

'Ready, everybody,' Randall said. 'Just do exactly as I say.'

The lift stopped. Randall walked out, his expression grim. Luca heard the shuffling of many feet somewhere out of sight. That wasn't good. He guessed they were in trouble. His sword was heavy against his chest, somehow sharpening his senses.

'Luca and Carter,' Randall said in a clear calm voice, 'I would like you to carry Mr Madoc out. Put him right here in front of me.'

They manhandled Madoc out of the lift, trying to avoid his squirms and kicks. A dozen armed men in black combats stared back at them.

'Good evening, gentlemen,' Randall said. 'As you can see, if you open fire you'll kill your boss. We're going to back away down this corridor. You, and by that I mean every one of you, are going to let us do that. If I see or hear so much as a sniff I'll put a bullet through him myself.'

'What's going on, sir? Explain.'

Luca glanced at the man who had spoken. He recognised the voice. It was the one who had led the massacre outside the Shard - the man who had killed Gwen's mum.

'With pleasure, Gabriel,' Randall replied. 'Madoc is my prisoner. He's a murderer. That's all there is to know. Now please be sensible and let us leave. Nobody needs to die here.'

'I can't let you go, sir,' Gabriel said. 'The secret alarm sounded. That means Mr Madoc is in danger.'

Gabriel's voice cracked slightly. Luca watched his trigger finger. It was shaking. That wasn't good.

'He was at Camelot,' Freddie said. 'He captured me and brought me here. I don't like him.'

'Secret alarm, Gabriel?' Randall said. 'Seems like I'm not the only one who's been hiding things.'

'Mr Madoc ordered me to install it. Good idea, by the look of it.'

'Luca, start moving the others back,' whispered Randall, a slight smile across his face. He looked as calm as a man browsing in a bookshop. 'Get behind me.'

Luca's heart was slamming. He was drenched in sweat. This was looking worse by the second.

Gabriel turned to his men. 'On my order, take them down.'

'No, Gabriel,' Randall shouted. 'We've done terrible things. This is your chance to do good for once.'

'These kids have brainwashed you, sir. They're using some of that fancy magic.'

'That's not true. I'm standing here of my own free will.' Randall lifted his sword from underneath his jacket. 'I've never been one of you. My true allegiance is to Camelot and the Pendragon.'

Gabriel shook his head.

'Have it your way, traitor.'

Luca guessed they were ten metres from a bend in the corridor. What chance all of them making it before the bullets hit? No chance at all. His mind raced, trying to decide what to do. He thought back to the hall and the incredible power of the swords. He had no idea how the swords had come to life like that, or how he had known that they might. He cursed Peake for telling them so little, and for all the secrets he had kept from them.

My dad would have told me everything, he thought.

Except he hadn't. The biggest secret of all was all of this, hidden from him all his life. Luca shook his head in frustration. It couldn't end here in a dumb corridor.

He shoved his hands into his pockets, trying to look brave. One of his fingers jabbed painfully against the edge of the photograph, folded and forgotten. His eyes widened.

You idiot, he told himself.

Be ready, his dad had written. Be smart. Believe, and follow your heart. It will always take you to the right place.

And that was what he had to do. It was time to stop doubting. It was time to be ready.

'The swords,' he said.

Luca held the tiny weapon so tightly he felt the jewel cut into his palm. He pointed it towards the others, ignoring Gabriel's curt order to adopt firing positions. Instead, Luca focused upwards. A familiar cold feeling trickled through his brain.

'With you,' Freddie said.

'Got it,' replied Carter.

The swords touched. Luca cried out, his hand suddenly burning. An enormous flash of light filled the corridor, brighter than anything he had ever seen before. The ceiling dissolved as a mass of steel and masonry collapsed down into the narrow space. Luca was hurled backwards. His ears were ringing and he struggled to breathe in the clogged air.

There were screams, muffled shouts, a gunshot, and then a strange kind of silence where the only sound was the rushing of blood in his head.

Finally, there was blackness.

35

'Gwen!'

She heard the shout from somewhere down a deep tunnel, or so it seemed. Her eyes and ears were full of fine dust. There was a horrible high-pitched buzzing sound all around her and she tasted something metallic. Her own blood, she guessed, although she couldn't be sure, because what she had seen the swords do was surely impossible.

Alarms were ringing and water was pouring down from the few remaining sprinklers. Gwen was quickly soaked, the dust washed away. She blinked a few times and sat up. Carter was calling her name. He crawled to her, checking her arms and legs, seeing if she was hurt.

'I'm okay,' she said. 'What about the others?'

They looked around. Red emergency lights had flicked on and the air was full of dirty mist. The corridor was a mess, completely blocked. She saw Luca down on the ground but he was moving. Freddie and Jess were staggering away from the debris. Their swords were still glowing in the gloom.

'That was amazing,' she said. Then she noticed Randall.

'Carter, help him!'

Randall was half buried beneath the rubble. He was groaning in pain and there was a wet bloom of dark blood across his chest. Her father was not there. Had he been buried? Had he managed to get away?

There wasn't time to worry about that. Randall was in a bad way. The children gathered around the stricken man. His eyes opened.

***

'Where's Madoc?' groaned Randall. 'And the vaccines - are they safe?'

Luca glanced down, his head clearing. The rucksack was lying in the wet dust.

'They're okay,' he said. 'Forget Madoc for a minute. We need to get you out of there. Can you move your legs?'

Randall shook his head.

'No. I'm trapped. I need to know if Madoc escaped.'

Luca didn't have an answer to that. It was all still a blur. The power from the swords had erupted with such intensity that it was as though the whole building was collapsing. Madoc could be anywhere. There was no sign of movement or noise from the other side of the blockage.

'Got to make sure he pays for what he's done, Luca. And you've got to get the vaccines out of here.'

Randall coughed. Pink froth bubbled up on his lips.

'Gabriel shot me.'

Luca glanced down at Randall's chest. The blood was spreading across his shirt.

'You need to save your energy. We'll get help. We can help.'

The words babbled from Luca but Randall lifted a weak hand to stop him.

'Too late. I've had it. Get out of here now - the job's not even half done yet.'

'I won't leave you.'

'Yes, you will.'

Luca slammed his fist down in frustration.

'First my dad,' he shouted. 'Then my mum and Peake. And now you. Everybody dies!'

Randall coughed and this time fresh blood bubbled up around his lips.

'Don't doubt yourself. Be strong. You're the Pendragon, aren't you?'

'Whatever that even means.'

'It means you've got...no choice but to do...what you know to be right.'

Luca nodded. He felt completely numb. Randall's eyes flickered and Luca felt his body sag.

'Hold on!' Luca shouted, blinking away the tears.

'More to tell you,' Randall whispered. He was fighting to get out the words. 'I have a son...Madoc never knew. You find him, okay? Give him my sword...he's one of you now.'

'A son? Where?'

'Canterbury.' Randall coughed up more blood. Every word was killing him. 'He's called George...he's hidden away...safe...'

He slumped back down. His chest was still, the blood-soaked sword gleaming dully against his skin. Randall was dead.

Luca slipped the sword from around the man's neck and placed it next to his own. He picked up the bag of vaccines and led his friends out of the ruined corridor into the stairwell. It was time to leave the Shard.

***

Bloodied and bruised, disoriented and confused, Madoc tried to sit up.

What happened? Am I alive? Is this...is this hell?

A voice was calling from somewhere a long way away. A man's voice. It was somehow familiar. The voice grew louder, shouting his name.

'Mr Madoc...Mr Madoc...Mr Madoc!'

Hands ripped the tape from his mouth and wrists. He rubbed at his eyes, grimacing at the pain. He blinked away the dust and blood.

'Who is it? Answer me, damn it.'

'It's Gabriel, sir,' the voice said.

Madoc focused on the man crouching over him.

'Gabriel,' he croaked. 'Of course.'

He tried to remember, searching his memory for anything that made sense.

'Randall!'

The single word came out like a curse.

'Update me. I want to know everything.'

Gabriel delivered a swift efficient summary. He seemed to be unaware of his own injuries. Madoc

201

noticed, for the first time, the half-buried bodies of his men.

'Just you and me, then,' he said, when Gabriel was finished.

'Yes, sir. And that sword you're holding – it shot out of Randall's pocket, like an arrow straight into your hands. Then you flew away from the explosion, like it was protecting you. I can't explain it.'

'No, I don't suppose you can,' Madoc said, feeling the familiar cold metal against his palm, and grateful for it.

Madoc pondered what he had heard. The power generated by the swords had been immense. For a second, a spasm of fear shot through him, but he pushed it away.

'Get down to the car park,' Madoc ordered. 'Contact every man left in the building and order them to meet us down there.'

'I shot Randall, sir,' said Gabriel. 'He must be dead.'

'Good man. Now go.'

Madoc stumbled after him.

I'm going to kill them all myself for this, he thought. And I'll enjoy every last moment.

36

The stairwell was full of dust but at least the sprinklers had stayed inactivated, and that meant no torrents of water and no slimy mud to slip on. They headed down quickly to the car park.

Fletcher was still there, moaning quietly. Carter ignored him and opened a box on the wall. It was full of keys and he grabbed a set at random. He pointed it at the vehicles and pressed the button. The lights of a nearby Range Rover flicked on and off.

'That one. Go,' shouted Carter.

'I suppose you can drive,' Luca said to Carter when they were in the vehicle.

'It's an automatic,' Carter replied. 'My brother showed me once. I reckon I can do it.'

'You'll need to get a move on,' Freddie called from the back seat. 'I can hear them coming.'

Fifty metres away, a fire door burst open and black-clad men spilled through into the car park. They didn't bother to shout a warning. Instead, bullets rattled off the vehicles all around them, sending hot sparks flying. They were thrown around inside as Carter accelerated up the ramp.

'Next stop the Tower!' Carter shouted.

They were gaining speed. The square of light at the top of the ramp was growing. Luca willed the car to go even faster, daring to believe they might make it, but then a burst of gunfire took out one of the back tyres. The Range Rover span out of control. It bounced off a wall, ripping away pipes and cables before wedging underneath the roller door at the top of the ramp. Luca fell forwards. Jess banged against a window and slumped down. Carter was struggling to get the car free but it was hopeless.

More gunfire slammed into the bodywork. Freddie pulled at Jess's sleeve but she was too dazed to notice. A nasty purple bruise was blooming above one eye.

'She can't hear me,' Freddie said. 'Her mind's closed.'

'Out of the way, Freddie,' shouted Gwen. 'Let me get her.'

The gunfire was almost constant. It was a matter of moments before one of them was hit. Gwen shoved Jess out, followed by Freddie. Luca acted without thinking. He threw himself onto the concrete and scrambled around to the front of the car, pulling Jess along. Carter joined them, the rucksack and book clutched to his chest.

'Can you use the swords?' Gwen asked, her voice nearly lost in the mayhem.

Luca shook his head. There was no spark from his, no feeling of it being alive. Whatever magic he had unleashed was gone, at least for now. Madoc's men were making steady progress up the ramp, moving expertly in groups, covering each other with long bursts of fire. And then Luca saw two figures emerge through the dust and darkness.

'It's Madoc and Gabriel.'

Madoc stood unafraid, his eyes wild. Luca glanced at Jess. She didn't look as dazed and was responding to Freddie's questions. He hoped she could run without too much help.

'She'll be okay,' Freddie said.

Then the shutter door started to whir and grind above them. Somebody must be trying to close it, except the roof of the car was holding it up. The vehicle groaned and shifted but the door's motor wasn't powerful enough to push the car out of the way. A new terrifying smell spread through the tunnel. One of those ripped pipes was leaking gas.

'It's going to explode,' Luca shouted. 'Get out!'

The five children hurled themselves into the street. Their legs and arms pumped. Every stride carried them that little bit further away from what was coming. A crowd had gathered nearby. A shout went up. The crowd pushed forwards, desperate for help. Then the gas ignited.

Luca's eardrums popped inwards and everything went very quiet. He half-turned and saw a fireball blossom out of the tunnel. The car and the roller door disappeared. Flames and black smoke spread up the building and out along the street.

Alarms were ringing everywhere. The heat was terrible, like standing too close to a Bonfire Night blaze. Their attackers must have been vaporised.

The crowd swayed back from the fire. Bodies lay crumpled and broken. The survivors screamed and ran, smashing into each other, knocking down the young and the sick. It was utter chaos.

Jess and Carter were nearby. Both were moving and that was the best Luca could hope for. The rucksack lay in the street - Luca had no idea about the book. Freddie and Gwen had been thrown further away and they were helping each other up, their clothes plastered in dust, their hair stuck out on end.

'Over here,' Luca screamed, his own voice muffled and echoing. 'And grab the bag!'

He had seen a chance for escape. The crowd could save them. The crowd would hide them.

***

'Give me an update,' Madoc barked at the wall-mounted screen in front of him. The service corridor was hot and smoky, but at least he was away from the fire raging behind the heavy iron door next to him.

A terrified looking man stared back at him. Madoc could see smoke drifting around in the control room. Twenty frustrating minutes had passed since the explosion. The whole building was catching fire. The man coughed out a quick message. They had people on the ground looking, he reassured his boss. The children wouldn't get far.

Madoc growled. Things weren't going to plan and that made him very angry indeed.

I had them in my grasp, he thought. The swords should be around my neck. Instead, I'm stuck here talking to this fool.

He turned to Gabriel, blackened with soot and blood.

'That was quick thinking when you smelled gas. Thank you. Now, how many men are still operational?'

'It was just luck that I got the fire door open, sir. I think there are forty or so left. The rest are dead or missing.'

Forty out of four hundred. Madoc fought back his anger, trying to stay calm.

'Get them out across London. Find those brats.'

'Yes, sir. We've managed to locate one of your Ducatis, undamaged.'

Madoc smiled grimly. On the motorbike, he could be at the Tower in a matter of minutes.

'It *will* happen, just like the book says.'

He gasped. How could he have forgotten the book? He punched the wall in frustration, trying to remember.

Yes. He had seen it just before the explosion. That cocky street kid had dropped it as he ran off. Fire couldn't damage it. Hadn't he kept it safe all these years underneath the flames in his office?

'Send somebody to the tunnel.'

'It's not safe, sir. There are still fires raging.'

'Find them protective clothing. Anything. There's a book in there that I need.'

'A book?'

'Yes! Don't question me. Get it, do you understand?'

'Of course, sir.'

Madoc swiped his hand across the screen and tapped in a code. Six red bars and one deep amber. The final raven was dying.

'I want my motorbike, Gabriel.'

'This way, sir.'

It took a while to find a way through the shattered building. Some corridors were blocked and they had to double back twice, but eventually Gabriel and Madoc emerged into the foyer. Two men were guarding a Ducati, machine guns ready. They stood to one side when Madoc approached. He climbed on and fired the engine.

'The Tower, Gabriel,' he shouted. 'Find out everything you can about routes in and out, then bring me the book. Don't fail me!'

Madoc didn't wait for an answer. He surged out of the Shard towards the shattered crowd. If they didn't move, he would mow them down.

37

'Keep together,' Luca shouted.

'I can't see you,' called Carter from somewhere behind. 'We're going to get split up.'

He was right. The surging crowd now numbered hundreds. They had to act quickly or it would be impossible to find each other again. There was a dark street off to his left.

'Head down there,' he mouthed at Jess.

She nodded. Freddie was already dipping towards it.

'Carter! Gwen!'

He ran forward and shouted as loudly as he could. There was no reply. Then he spotted a man staring at him. He looked different from the rest of the crowd – lean and fit, cold eyed. The man lifted his wrist up to his mouth. He was talking into something.

Luca ducked down and swerved left. He risked another look. The man now had his back to him, still searching, but the crowd was serving its purpose by keeping Luca hidden.

'Over here, mate.'

Carter's voice was close and he jumped as a hand landed on his shoulder.

'Got you,' said Carter, roughly pulling Luca into the doorway of a café. Gwen was there with him, lurking in the shadows.

'There's a few of Madoc's boys out there,' said Carter. 'We managed to get here without being spotted.'

'I saw one.'

'We need to get under cover. Where are the others?'

Carter pushed away a woman who staggered against him. Her face was filthy and her hair was a tangled mess. She smelled terrible.

'I sent them down the next side street.'

'Good stuff. Let's go and join them. Then we need to head along the river. If we can lose them we'll try and cross Tower Bridge and cut back from there.'

'How far's that?' Luca asked.

'Maybe a mile.'

'What about London Bridge?' asked Gwen. 'It would get us over the river quicker.'

'No,' Carter said. 'Too open. And it's what they'll expect us to do. Luca?'

'This is your town. We do what you say.'

They pushed their way back into the crowd, staying close to each other, keeping low to avoid being spotted. They were moving against the tide of people but eventually they broke through into the side street.

'Freddie?' whispered Luca.

Luca looked around but there was nothing to see except deep shadows and piles of rubbish.

'Here.'

Freddie stepped out from behind a car.

'I heard you coming a mile off,' he said.

'That's because you've got a weird radar in your head.'

Freddie grinned.

'I know. And it's still working. I can hear men talking about us. They're coming this way.'

'Follow me,' Carter said, already picking up speed.

***

'Nearly there,' shouted Carter, urging them on. Luca glanced across the river and saw the Tower of London for the first time. It was dwarfed by the gleaming buildings behind it, but there was no mistaking its solidity and power.

It'll be okay, he thought. The girl will be there.

'Are they still following us, Freddie?' Luca asked.

'Yes. Not going to let us go, are they?'

'Fair enough. Dumb question.'

He looked at Jess. Her eyes were dark and her breathing was coming in great big rasps, but there was a look of grim determination on her face. He wanted to hold her and tell her all the things he felt.

Maybe later, he thought. If there is a later.

Gwen was glued to Carter's side as always. All of their steps were synchronised - they were a team, each one of them ready to do whatever was necessary. Then, from somewhere behind them, gunfire chattered. Hot tarmac flew up around their ankles.

'Go!' shouted Carter. 'Under there!'

He was pointing at an archway off the embankment. More shots cracked out. One bullet missed Luca's trailing heel by no more than ten centimetres. They ran through winding streets and back alleys before Carter looped them back towards the river. And then they were approaching Tower Bridge.

***

Madeleine stood facing the glass cabinet in the armoury. The strange floating sword was shining, its black diamond gleaming like oil. She held up her own sword. The two tiny weapons hummed in sequence, like instruments tuning up with each other.

The door opened and McKenna barrelled through.

'There's trouble across the river. Shots fired.' His face was glowing with excitement. 'Five kids running this way.'

Madeleine smiled.

'They're here.'

38

The wind howled around Tower Bridge's immense bulk as they drew near. Luca glanced back. The Shard seemed to loom over them like a malevolent monster. A ball of fire belched up the side of the building and the top disappeared behind greasy smoke as the whole structure let out a low desperate groan.

Let it burn down, he thought. And I hope Madoc's still inside when it falls.

They moved forward cautiously, expecting an attack at any moment. They were soon in the middle of the bridge, with the wind buffeting them. Luca paused.

'Careful,' Jess murmured next to him. 'I don't like this.'

Before Luca could reply, an armed man jumped out in front of them.

'Stop! All of you, hands up and move slowly towards me. I'll shoot the first one who tries anything stupid.'

There was no choice but to do as he said. They raised their hands and walked across the bridge.

'Gotcha,' the man said. 'Back to Mr Madoc, kids.'

'Not a chance.'

Gwen launched herself like a cobra. The first kick caught the man on the bridge of the nose. The second slammed against his forehead. He made a horrible gurgling noise and his gun fired.

They all ducked, Gwen dropping almost to her knees with her hands outstretched. For a sickening moment, Luca thought she had been shot. Then she attacked again. One hand sliced into the side of the man's neck. The other hand dragged him forwards. Her knee drove into his chest and he collapsed.

'Cool,' said Freddie. 'Like a Power Ranger. Or Harley Quinn. I like her.'

'Let's get off the bridge,' Gwen gasped.

'Too late,' said Carter. 'Another one above us. We're sitting ducks.'

It was the perfect ambush. Luca closed his eyes and waited for the bullets to hit.

A shot did ring out, but it came from some distance away. Luca heard a muffled scream and then the gunman smashed down onto the road with a wet thud. A loudspeaker crackled from the direction of the Tower and a deep voice boomed out.

'Get across as fast as you can!'

A flare exploded above the ramparts. A row of lamps burst into life, illuminating the ancient wall and the two figures waving at them. One was a man dressed in some kind of old fashioned uniform. The other was tiny next to him - she had long red hair.

'You,' Luca whispered.

The children ran with every remaining ounce of energy they had. Nothing else mattered. They skidded up the ramp into the Tower, then they were inside. The

214

huge wooden portcullis slammed down seconds after the children stumbled through.

'Welcome to the Tower,' said the uniformed man, 'but I don't suppose you're in the mood for the official tour.'

Luca fell down onto the wet cobbles, gasping for breath. Somehow they had made it. Now that they were inside the Tower, the adrenaline drained away like water down a plughole.

'You all right, son?'

The man leaned down and stared at Luca.

'I think so.'

'Good lad. That was some running. Made my job that bit easier. Any idea how many of them are after you?'

Luca shook his head, unable to speak.

'Fair enough. Don't suppose you were stopping to count. Anyway, you made it. Welcome to the Tower of London. My name's Sam McKenna. I'm the Ravenmaster.'

'And I'm Madeleine. Hello.'

Luca looked up at the girl with red hair. She gave him a shy smile. She was holding an old cuddly toy, some kind of grubby ladybird.

'Oh...you're, um...I expected...' the words were all wrong. He knew that. He tried again. 'You're...'

'She's my niece,' McKenna said, cutting across him. 'She's got Down's syndrome, okay?'

215

His voice was clipped and stern. Don't argue with me, that voice said. Don't even think about questioning me. Luca swallowed hard.

'Yeah. Okay. Hello.'

'This is Hug-a-Bug,' the girl said. 'He likes you.'

Freddie stepped forwards, his head cocked sideways, peering at Madeleine as if he was examining a laboratory specimen.

'That's cool. I can't read her. Like a locked box, or something. Anyway, have you got any chocolate? I'm starving.'

***

In the Ravenmaster's office, Freddie reached for another toffee.

'These are the best,' he said, chewing and grinning at the same time. 'How did I never know about Riesens?'

'My favourite,' Madeleine replied, staring at him. 'Don't eat them all, though.'

'Didn't think you'd ever get here,' McKenna said. 'But Madeleine knew otherwise.'

'There's lots of stuff happened that won't make any sense,' said Luca.

McKenna laughed.

'You'd be surprised, son. Not exactly been Normal Street here.'

'We've brought vaccines against the plague. Any idea how we get them to somebody who might know what to do with them?'

'As a matter of fact, I do. My brother works for the government. He's a virologist. That's a kind of scientist who studies viruses and infections. We can get that bag to him. His laboratory is underneath the Gherkin building, the big curved thing not far from here,' he said, addressing Luca. 'It's a secret place where the government's best scientists work. Nobody knows about it, but it's there. We haven't always got on, Jim and me. When Madeleine was born...well, let's just say I struggled with it. Soldiers are better at actions than with words. And I didn't much care for his wife...Madeleine's mum.'

'Mummy's dead,' Madeleine said in a quiet voice. 'Daddy said I would be safe here.'

She looked at her uncle. McKenna smiled at her and squeezed her hand.

'You are, my darlin'.'

She's been like a dream, Luca thought, and now she's standing in front of me. I know her and I don't. I expected someone different...

'You brought me here,' he said, smiling at her, hoping to make a connection. 'That's a special thing to do.'

'I'm just me,' Madeleine replied.

'Yeah. We're all a bit odd, to be honest.' Luca cringed. 'Sorry. Not saying you're...I mean...'

Jess stepped forwards and took Madeleine's hands, sparing Luca's embarrassment.

'What he's trying to say, is that you're one of us.'

Madeleine looked at Luca.

'What's your name?'

'Luca. That's Freddie, Jess, Carter. And Gwen.'

'She doesn't have a sword,' she said.

'No,' interrupted Luca, unsure what else to say. 'Gwen's...she's not...'

Carter spoke for him.

'Gwen doesn't need a sword.'

'Okay,' Madeleine shrugged. 'Luca's the Pendragon. I heard that in my head.'

'So everybody keeps telling me,' Luca replied. 'Do you know who you are? I mean, which knight was your ancestor?'

Madeleine looked puzzled.

'King Arthur talks to him,' Carter explained. 'I've seen the round table. You know, normal stuff like that.'

Madeleine didn't seem to find Carter's joke funny. Luca tried again.

'Madeleine, we've got loads to tell you, but I don't think we've got time.'

'You're right,' she said. 'It's taken you ages to get here.'

Gwen stepped forwards, looking directly at McKenna.

'You said swords - there's more than one here?'

'Yes. The one around Madeleine's neck and one floating all by itself next to the Black Prince's armour.'

'Who?'

'Edward of Woodstock. He was a Plantagenet, fourteenth century.'

Luca tried to work it out, remembering what Peake had said. The Plantagenet kings were descended from Arthur. The Black Prince was one of them. It was all coming together.

'It's beautiful, with a big black diamond,' continued Madeleine.

Luca's skin crawled. Madoc's sword had the same.

'And not one of us has gone down with the plague,' said McKenna, interrupting his thoughts. 'I, uh, I think the swords are protecting us.'

Luca looked at the old soldier to see if he was joking, but the man's eyes were hard and cold.

'I think you're right. How many of you are there?' Luca asked him.

'Thirty eight.'

'I hope it's enough.'

McKenna paused, weighing up Luca's statement.

'Depends on who's coming after you.'

'John Madoc. He released the plague. Those are his men out there. They won't stop. We escaped from the Shard, and we...' Luca paused. The whole story would have to wait. 'Never mind. He wants the swords and he wants us dead.'

'Madoc?' McKenna whistled. 'Always thought he looked a shifty character.'

'He's Gwen's dad,' Freddie replied.

'Well, now. That complicates things a bit. So we need to get these vaccines to the Gherkin and keep you kids safe? I'm sure a bunch of idiots like us can manage that. First, let's get you other kids fed and watered.' He glanced at Freddie, still chewing on a toffee. 'An army fights on its stomach. And then you can tell me everything.'

39

'Mr McKenna,' Luca said, his voice low, 'how can you believe any of this?'

McKenna put down his mug and rubbed at his chin. The canteen was noisy and chaotic. The children were dotted around, trying their best to explain it all to the Warders.

'Good question, son. All this stuff you've just told me...well, why not? And look at Madeleine. I've always thought there was something special about that kid. Take that sword she's wearing. She says a raven gave it her. He talked to her!'

Luca thought of Bran. He wished the bird was there with him, clacking and chattering, and he wondered for a moment if he might have brought the sword to Madeleine. Why not? Anything was possible.

'And the other sword hanging in the White Tower just appeared out of nowhere,' McKenna continued. 'Now, when you've been a soldier as many years as me, you've seen lots of mad things. This is just another one. It's like Madeleine's suddenly in charge, you know? And one thing us soldiers are good at is following orders.'

'My dad was in the army.'

'Good for him.' McKenna paused. 'You said he *was*.'

'He got killed in Afghanistan. I was only six.'

McKenna's tough face softened.

'I'm sorry,' he said, his tone more gentle. 'I fought there myself. Scary place, sometimes.'

'I can't really remember him,' Luca added, hoping his voice wasn't going to crack in front of everybody. 'Just bits, like the way he used to pull a funny face when he told a joke.'

'Well,' said McKenna, 'from what I've seen, I reckon he'd be a proud dad today.'

For a moment, time slowed to nothing. Each of them stood thinking of what they had lost and what could still be. Luca took out the photograph. It was torn and dirty, but his dad's words were still clear.

'He looks solid enough,' McKenna said. 'And your mum's a good looking lady.'

'Yeah. I miss them.'

'That's enough of that,' sniffed McKenna, wiping his nose. 'I'm too tough to be crying.'

Just then, another Warder came into the canteen. He was nearly as tall as McKenna, but stockier and older.

'Sir,' he said, 'you need to come quick. He's going downhill. I don't think he's got long.'

'Thank you, Mr Morgan. We're on our way.'

The place fell silent. McKenna stood up and headed straight for the door.

'What's going on?' Luca asked.

'It's the final raven,' McKenna replied. 'He's dying.'

***

Madoc skidded to a halt. The Ducati's powerful engine hummed as he surveyed the wreckage of the

Tower complex. The tourist shops were smashed in. Everything had been looted. He stared at the famous old castle. It was enormous, and for the briefest of moments he felt a tiny flicker of doubt. Could he really achieve what so many of his ancestors had failed to do?

No time for that, he thought. I'm a Madoc. I can do anything.

One of his men approached.

'Five children were seeing going in, sir.'

'My daughter.'

'Yes, sir. We've got plastic explosives ready. What are your orders?'

'Get into the Tower.'

The man paused.

'What are you waiting for?' Madoc said quietly.

'As soon as we know it's safe to go in, we will.'

Madoc slammed his fist against the side of the motorbike.

'Attack now! Go!'

The man blinked once, then nodded.

'Yes, sir. And your daughter? What do we do with Gwendoline?'

He thought of her, back in the Shard. She had looked different, with cold eyes and a hardness in her limbs. His daughter had been replaced by a tiger who would kill him, given the chance. He smiled, almost proud of her. Then he pushed the emotion away. It was too late for that. Much too late.

'Kill her. Kill them all.'

Madoc reached for his phone. Gabriel answered immediately.

'Yes, sir.'

'They've managed to get into the Tower. The vaccines aren't any use stuck in there, so they'll have to look for another way out.'

'That's been dealt with,' replied Gabriel. 'I've studied old plans of the Tower and identified a tunnel running out onto the north side. It comes up at street level.'

'Get there. Take any spare men you can find. Cover the whole area. I'm on my way.'

'And Mr Madoc, we've got the book. Two men died in the recovery, but it's unharmed.'

'My condolences to their families. Bring it with you.'

Madoc ended the call and sat quietly on the motorbike, thinking it through. He had the book. Good. Something was nagging at his brain – something he was missing.

'No,' he whispered, suddenly alert to a new possibility.

He switched the phone back on. The screen told its own story, a deep orange bar flickering into red. Nothing could save the final raven, not even...

Madoc gulped. A trickle of sweat ran down his back as he recalled the ceiling crashing down onto his men. Could the swords stop the bird dying?

He suddenly felt an anxiety that angered him more than the children's escape. They would soon be inside the

Tower, but Madoc suspected it needed to be even quicker than that. It needed to be now.

Madoc checked his phone once more. The raven was weakening, and he noticed the sky was growing heavy. A storm was coming from the north but it was no natural phenomenon. Merlin's spell book was very clear on that. Whatever was left after the storm passed...well, he would soon know once the last bar turned red.

As he gunned the engine, the first heavy drops of rain splattered onto the cobbles and the wind picked up in an unearthly howl.

The ancient spell was beginning.

40

The White Tower was filled with priceless artefacts, weaponry and displays going back over hundreds of years of history. They paused by the Black Prince's armour. The sword hovered in front of them.

'It's just like ours,' Carter said.

'Yeah,' replied Luca. 'But who does it belong to now?'

Gwen was next to him. She shivered and turned away.

'I don't like that sword. It feels wrong, somehow. It's...'

She turned away and buried her face in Carter's shoulder, who looked confused but quietly pleased. He wrapped his arms around her.

'I can feel something coming from it,' said Jess. 'I can hear a voice calling to...'

The sword glowed for a second but Gwen slammed her hand against the cabinet. The glow instantly faded.

'I don't want to know,' she said.

There was no time to argue because McKenna shouted at them to hurry up. They followed him and Morgan deeper into the ancient building until they reached a windowless room. Another Warder was there, leaning over a long wooden trough. A raven was lying on a makeshift bed of coats and blankets.

'That's Sergeant Major Jarvis,' said McKenna. 'He's looking after the bird, making sure he's comfortable.

'I don't know why I brought him here,' said Jarvis, 'but it seemed the right thing to do.'

'Because he's the final raven,' Freddie replied, 'and we're the children of Camelot.'

Jarvis looked at the boy.

'I just felt...something in my head.'

'Yeah,' Luca interrupted. 'You felt *him*.'

'He can read my mind?' asked Jarvis.

Nobody answered. McKenna and Jarvis exchanged a glance.

'These are the kids Madeleine told us about.'

There was a new edge to McKenna's voice, a realisation that something way beyond his comprehension was happening. Jarvis was a small wiry man. His eyes were red as if he had been crying.

'I hope you can explain all that to me soon,' Jarvis said. 'And I'm sorry we're not meeting in happier circumstances. I think he's nearly gone.'

The raven's wings were unfolded and his beak opened slowly, as if he was trying to suck in more air. Luca reached out and touched the bird. The heart beat was barely there, like a fluttering dream. He remembered how strong Bran had felt, with his muscled chest and quivering wing feathers. This bird was a ghost in comparison.

I could really do with him here now, he thought. And Peake, and my mum and dad. I miss them all so much.

McKenna looked close to tears. When he spoke, his voice was thick with emotion.

'I love my ravens.'

Luca understood exactly what the Ravenmaster meant.

'There's an ancient spell, you know,' Luca whispered. 'When he dies, Britain's lost.'

McKenna smiled in spite of his anguish.

'Just a myth, Luca. An old Victorian tale embroidered over the years.'

'No,' Luca replied, the frustration bubbling up in him like a boiling kettle. 'That's the point. It's not a myth, it's a real spell that was placed on the Tower by Merlin. He's called Peake now, remember? It's all just like I told you in the canteen. Madeleine saw him in her dream. He gathered us all together at Camelot, but he didn't tell us everything. He left us to find most of it for ourselves.'

The words tumbled from him, a rapid explosion of thoughts as he tried to make sense of everything.

'That's what all of this is about, and John Madoc's part of the same story.'

The three old soldiers stood in silence, staring at Luca as he spoke. He punched his forehead in frustration.

'You want to hear it again? It's just like Freddie said. We're the children of Camelot.'

Luca's head dropped. He didn't have the energy to say more. He just wanted to fall asleep in his own bed. He wanted all this to go away.

'And Luca's the last descendent of King Arthur,' whispered Jess. 'He's the Pendragon.'

'Yep. If the raven dies,' Freddie said in his usual calm way, 'then there won't be any left.'

The bird's eyes were glazed, as if it was staring off into some unseen distance.

Please don't die, thought Luca. Not just because of the spell, but because I don't want you to.

'This is for real?' Jarvis asked. 'Merlin, spells, all that stuff?'

'A few days ago, I'd have laughed with you,' Luca replied. 'It's real. Every bit of it.'

Luca stroked the raven. It lifted its head to him, wings flapping with something like desperation.

'Then if he's going to die, son,' McKenna said, 'it sounds like we've already lost.'

Luca frowned. 'No. Not yet.'

Believe, Peake had told him. His mum had said the same. His dad had written it down in case he never saw him again.

Believe...believe...

I do, Luca thought.

Everything so far had been leading up to this moment. He was ready to be the Pendragon. He turned to the others. His face was grim, but determined.

'We're friends, aren't we?'

Carter nodded.

'Too right.'

'Best ones I ever had,' added Gwen, her voice cracking.

'And the love bit...that's what we need to do now. We need to love this bird as much as the Ravenmaster.'

'I can do that,' said Freddie.

'We all can,' Jess replied. 'We all do. I know we do.'

'Then lift up your swords and help him,' Luca urged. 'Think about all of the ravens on Lundy. And think about Bran.'

Carter's sword was up in the air, the first hint of light glowing around its edge. Jess lifted hers. So did Freddie and Luca. The four swords were held over the dying bird like a guard of honour. Luca turned to Madeleine.

'I know you weren't there in Camelot, and your sword hasn't touched the Round Table, but we might need it anyway.'

Her sword joined theirs. Gwen reached down and stroked the great bird's head.

'I'm sorry I can't help,' she said.

As she finished speaking, the room started to rumble as if a train was passing. The floor shook. Puffs of ancient cement floated off the walls. The door flew

230

open. A huge ball of light filled Luca's vision and he fell backwards.

Somebody screamed - it might have been him. The noise and light was too intense to know. Madeleine's hand gripped him like a vice. That helped, because he wanted to run, to get away from the sound of the screaming.

'Believe!' Luca shouted. 'We've got to believe!'

Then the noise was gone. The room was black. The only sound was the thudding of his heart.

'It can't be,' Gwen said.

The light returned but it was softer than before. The raven was lit up like a star, bathed in magical, impossible light. Shadows of other birds flitted around the room, then were gone. Luca imagined Bran here, calling out and flapping his wings. And then he stared in disbelief – the Black Prince's sword was in Gwen's hand.

'Gwen *is* one of us,' Jess said. 'I understood that earlier, by the cabinet. When your mum died, you must have become the last of the line. Don't you see? You're a child of Camelot too!'

'Oh, priceless,' laughed Carter. 'Madoc's own daughter, one of us. Wouldn't I love to see him know that.'

Luca's brain almost ached with it all, but at that moment only the final raven mattered. The swords slowly grew cooler again and the light died away. Finally the room was dark, and deathly silent.

Jarvis rubbed a hand across his eyes as if to convince himself of what he had just seen. He touched the bird's chest. He shone a torch into one eye, then the other. He turned to face Luca.

'No good, son. Nothing's changed. He's nearly gone.'

'It can't be,' shouted Luca. 'It must have worked. The swords are all we've got. Peake made me promise!'

Jarvis shook his head. Luca felt utterly empty. It had all been for nothing.

'That's it then,' said McKenna. 'You tried. I don't know what I just saw, but you did your best.'

As he spoke, an enormous explosion outside shook the room. A few panes of ancient glass smashed onto the floor. McKenna ran to the damaged window and looked down. His face was grave.

'Madoc's men have blown their way in. They're coming this way.'

***

Luca slumped down, broken and desolate. He had truly believed the swords would save the raven.

I'm useless, he thought. They all believed in me and I've done nothing.

He wanted to run from the room, away from it all. Freddie walked over to him. His green eyes were narrowed, as if he was thinking hard about something. Luca felt the familiar cold crawl in his head.

'Go away,' he said. 'Leave me alone.'

'We still have to deliver the vaccines, Luca.'

'The raven's going to die,' he replied bitterly. 'What's the point?'

Luca stared at the battered rucksack, speckled with Randall's blood. Before he could speak again, Gwen made the decision for him.

'You and me, Luca, looks like we're part of the same thing. That means we never give up. Maybe we can save little Josh. Maybe your mum. Maybe we can save thousands of people.'

'Come on, mate,' urged Carter. 'You're not a quitter.'

Luca looked from one to the other, these fantastic friends who still believed. He thought of his dad, and what he would have done.

'You're right,' he said. 'We get those vaccines where they need to go.'

41

'Jim,' said McKenna into his ancient brick Nokia, 'I've got something special for you. Be ready. Madeleine's fine. She's on her way.'

He ended the call.

'There's a secret tunnel system under the Tower,' he said. 'Only a few of us know about it. You can use it to escape.'

'And you, uncle Sam,' Madeleine said.

'No, darlin'. My place is here with the rest of my men and with that raven. Morgan and Jarvis will take you. I want to be here when...when he dies...'

His words trailed away.

'Leave it to us,' Morgan said. 'We'll deliver the vaccines, simple as that.'

'Take the tunnel from the old chapel,' muttered McKenna. 'You'll come out near Tower Hill tube station. Make your way up to street level and go to the Gherkin. And look after these kids, you hear me?'

Morgan held out a hand and McKenna took it.

'Think this might be goodbye, Sam.'

McKenna nodded.

'Think you're right.'

His voice cracked with emotion and his eyes glistened with tears. Madeleine ran up to him and buried her face in the folds of his cloak. Hug-a-Bug tumbled to the floor. The old soldier carefully picked the soft toy up and tucked it into Madeleine's pocket.

'Be careful,' he said. 'Now go. Please.'

Bursts of automatic fire rattled the air outside. They heard shouts, then screams. A battle was raging for control of the Tower. The time for talking was over.

***

They followed Morgan at speed. Gwen struggled to believe she was a child of Camelot too. It would take more than a sword for her to really feel she was like the others. Taking the vaccine from her father was just the beginning. She knew until it was delivered, the job wasn't done. Carter held her hand as they ran, but she sensed he was wary. Everything was changing so quickly.

'So are we cousins or something?' Carter muttered. 'Too weird.'

'We're not cousins, you idiot,' she smiled. 'I'm still just me.'

They were in the stark Norman chapel, their footsteps echoing against the ancient flagstones. There was a small grate set in the floor. Morgan heaved it to one side and pointed into the stinking darkness.

'Get down the hole, Jarvis,' Morgan said.

'Why do I go first?'

'Because you're a lean mean fighting machine and I'm...well, I'm more of a comfortable sofa kind of bloke. You get the bullet and I get the medal. Fair enough?'

'Fair enough, you idiot,' said Jarvis, grinning at his friend.

He climbed in, feet first. The others followed. They descended quickly using iron rungs set into the wall as a ladder. After ten claustrophobic metres they were standing in a long passage.

Water dripped down onto them and the floor was slippery with algae and a thick layer of what Gwen suspected was rat droppings. She lifted her feet a little higher. Jarvis flashed torchlight across the ancient brickwork, his pistol held up ready to fire if necessary.

After twenty sweaty minutes of shuffling along a tunnel that sloped downwards the whole way, they reached another shaft. Gwen stared up. It was easily three times longer than the one they had just climbed down. A head for heights was going to be needed.

I won't look down, she thought. If I do...

Gwen recalled something that Randall had drilled into her during the long painful sessions of self-defence.

Bravery isn't the lack of fear, he would say. It's when you confront your fear.

'Randall was very brave,' whispered Freddie.

Gwen jumped.

'I heard what you were thinking. Sorry. And you're not a murderer. You're my friend.'

Before she had a chance to reply, Morgan was on the bottom rung.

'Up we go,' he grunted. 'Unfit old soldiers first.'

There wasn't time to argue. They started to climb.

***

It seemed to take forever. The iron rungs bit into Gwen's palms but she knew she had to keep going. She gritted her teeth and wiped the sweat from her eyes. It was such a long way up. Gwen just hoped she could hold on all the way.

'Nearly there,' Morgan called down to them.

Gwen rested her forehead against the rungs. She could hear Morgan struggling to push open the manhole cover at the top of the shaft. Then a loud scraping noise echoed around as the cover moved and fresh air rushed in, together with cold stinging rain.

They were moving again. She took another deep breath and started to climb. Jarvis was only a few feet ahead of her. Morgan cursed as he scrambled up onto the street. Gwen tensed herself, ready for an attack, but none came. His head popped back down into the shaft.

'Looks deserted. Quick, all of you. We need to get a shift on.'

Morgan ignored their protests of tiredness. He wanted them out of sight. So, less than a minute after they cleared the lip of the shaft and flopped onto the tarmac, they were off again.

They ran up Trinity Square, past deserted hotels and shuttered restaurants. The sky was slate grey above the buildings. The rain was so cold, Gwen's face was numb in seconds and her hands glowed red with pain. Northumberland Avenue narrowed to a thin alleyway into Fenchurch Street and then they were on Aldgate. The wind howled. The rain was coming down in thick sheets, soaking everything. The Gherkin was straight ahead of them, no more than fifty metres away.

'Come on,' shouted Morgan. 'Follow me.'

He didn't get a chance to say any more. As he ran forwards, a single shot rang out. He fell and lay still like a pile of crumpled washing.

'No!'

Jarvis yelled and dashed towards his friend but a second shot clipped the ground. He skidded backwards, pushing the children with him.

'Ambush - they've got ahead of us!'

42

Jarvis gathered them together, urging them to keep down. The bag of vaccines lay exposed in the street, next to Morgan's lifeless body. Luca tried to push past but Jarvis blocked his way.

'No way, son. You'd be shot down in a second.'

'We can't just sit here,' Luca said. 'We've got to get that bag.'

'See what just happened?' Jarvis asked, his eyes cold and focused.

'Yeah. I'm sorry about your mate.'

'He was a good soldier. Now do as I say.'

'Okay.'

Good lad. I think there's only one shooter. He'll wait for the next one of us to try it. We need a diversion. Something to draw his fire.'

He pointed at an abandoned car twenty metres away.

'Something like that. Stay here.'

He scuttled off, head down, weaving side to side. He slid in by the driver's door and looked in. Then he ran back, holding up the car's keys like a winning lottery ticket.

'I can drive it straight up the street. He won't be able to resist a nice big juicy target like that. It'll give you kids a chance to grab the bag and sprint for the Gherkin. Use me as cover.'

'That's a plan?' Carter interrupted. 'Bloody hell, mate. He'll hit you with everything they've got.'

'Maybe,' grinned Jarvis. 'Or maybe I'll be lucky. Then I can park it neatly and wait for you to arrive.'

'Let's do it.'

Carter was already in position, eyeing up the distance to the bag.

'Wait until I've drawn their fire,' Jarvis said, his voice suddenly flat and urgent. 'Spread out. Keep moving. Confuse them. I'll swerve around as best I can to cover you.'

Jarvis quickly patted each of them on the back.

'Morgan had one more medal than me. This is my chance to catch him up.'

And he was off, sprinting for the car.

'Get ready,' said Luca. 'I'll go for the bag. The rest of you do as Jarvis said.'

'What, and let you take a bullet?' Carter replied. 'No way. I'll get it.'

The car spluttered into life. The gears engaged with a horrible grind. Jarvis revved the engine and lurched the vehicle forwards. Then he was building up speed and roaring past them, giving them a thumbs up as he went by. Luca didn't hesitate.

'Go!'

And before Carter could stop him, he was running towards the vaccines.

'Come back, you idiot!'

Luca ignored Carter's shouts. He focused on the bag, counting each step as he ran, heart pounding, legs pumping. He was protected behind the car. Bullets were already pinging into the side of it. Luca swept up the bag and kept running. Out of the corner of his vision he saw black shapes darting towards him.

More than one, then.

He didn't have far to go. The Gherkin was up ahead. He could see men inside, waving at him. His chest was on fire. He could taste metal in his mouth. Nothing was going to stop him.

A loud burst of automatic fire hit the car. Luca stumbled and swerved. The car's brakes squealed and the engine roared. He risked a glance. Jarvis was slumped over the steering wheel. There was blood on the shattered windows. The car smashed straight into a shop front, crushing two of Madoc's men at the same time.

You'll get that medal, Luca thought.

He swerved again, dropping his shoulders, willing his muscles to give him more. A horrible burning pain slashed across his thigh, and he was down on the ground. He was twenty metres away from the doors. He struggled back to his feet. Ten metres, then he was down again.

'Give me the bag!'

Gwen's voice rang out clearly. His head buzzed. He touched the bullet wound. His hand came away sticky and hot with blood.

'They shot me.'

'Luca, the bag!'

He threw it towards her. She caught it cleanly and ran on. Bullets chipped the tarmac around her, but it seemed to Luca that nothing could stop her now. She was at the doors, banging hard against the glass. They slid open.

We win, Luca thought.

Not yet.

Jess was in his head, warm and soothing. The pain was suddenly less. He wanted to argue but he couldn't find the words. His eyes closed.

'I'm so tired,' he said. 'I could sleep for a week.'

Stay with me, Jess whispered, her words drifting through him like soft clouds. *Lots to do.*

Luca forced himself awake. He risked a look at his leg, surprised by how much blood there was. And why could he hear lots of shouting?

It was a man in a white lab coat. The vaccine bag hung by his side.

'Look behind you!'

'Daddy,' Madeleine gasped, almost falling over Luca in her haste to get to the doors but it was too late. Madoc's men seemed to be everywhere. The rain grew heavier, if that was possible. Gabriel ran up to Luca, his machine gun pointed directly at Luca's head. He was filthy with soot and dust and there was blood across his face, but he was very much alive.

242

'That's far enough, thanks,' Gabriel said. 'Mr Madoc, they're all yours.'

A shadowy figure emerged. It was Madoc, the skull sword hanging loosely around his neck. He cradled the spell book in his arms.

'Hello, Pendragon,' he said. 'Welcome to the end of the world.'

***

'Keep walking!'

Gabriel shoved the barrel of his machine gun into Luca's back, pushing him on. The bullet wound in his leg had stopped bleeding, but the pain was a constant grind. He did his best not to limp. He didn't want to give anybody the satisfaction of seeing him hurting.

'What's the hurry? You're going to shoot us as soon as we get back to the Tower.'

Another jab, this time into the ribs. Luca stumbled. He breathed deeply, fighting back the urge to lash out. Madoc turned and grinned.

'Not going so well now, my friend. And that tunnel you so kindly showed me...very helpful. I imagine my men are already in control.'

He was almost dancing with excitement. The Tower was ahead. The mean wind coming off the river cut through their clothes like knives as they were roughly halted under the walls. The children shivered in a tight huddle.

'So, are you all ready to die?'

Madeleine squeezed Luca's arm.

'He's scary,' she said. 'I don't like him at all.'

'Neither do I.'

'We've got the swords. We could make them shine again.'

'Why? They didn't save the final raven.'

'No, they didn't,' said Madoc, clearly enjoying every moment, and Luca had never felt more lost. He lowered his head, unwilling to look at any of his friends. He didn't want his pain mirrored in their eyes.

'The bird's dying,' Madoc continued. 'It'll soon be dead. And you lot have caused me no end of trouble, you know. The Shard's burning down. You stole the vaccines. And my motorbikes...have you any idea how much I loved those bikes? No, of course not. But never mind, because I've won.'

Gabriel held out his phone. Six bars were red. The seventh was a deep orange.

'Putting up a fight in there, I'll give it that. But any second now, all the ravens will be dead.'

Madoc opened the book and began to read. His voice was urgent and raw, as if he couldn't get the words out quickly enough. The wind was roaring around them. Luca ducked as a cardboard box flashed past. More debris swirled in the freezing air. If this was really the end, it wasn't going to be pleasant. Madoc looked up, his eyes staring.

'Can you feel it building? The final reading, as the final raven dies!'

He focused his attention on the book.

'The storm arrives and the raven dies,' he chanted. 'The storm arrives and the raven dies...the raven dies...the raven dies!'

Madoc threw his head back and laughed. It was a horrible sound. Luca understood at that moment that the man was completely and utterly insane.

43

Luca didn't know what ignited his anger. Was it the pain, or the cold, or the sense of injustice that burned in him? Did it matter? Not really. All that mattered was how he felt.

We were so close, he thought. We got the vaccines to Madeleine's dad. We should be in there, warm and laughing, cheering, doing all the things that winners do. We haven't failed...we haven't failed...we can't fail...

But they had. The evidence was all around him - the others with their heads down, cold and beaten. The wind and rain growing into something beyond comprehension. The Tower looming over them, and inside the final raven clinging to life because the swords hadn't been enough to save it. He slumped to his knees, defeated.

Stay calm...I can feel something coming...

Luca blinked, surprised at how loud Jess's voice was in his head. He glanced across. Her eyes were closed and she was concentrating hard. What was it?

Madoc was shouting and screaming, waving his arms around in lunatic windmills of excitement. He was no longer saying actual words. He was too far gone in his madness for that.

'I hate you so much,' Luca said, even though he knew Madoc couldn't hear him. 'I wish you were dead.'

Madoc did seem to pause, just for a moment. Luca saw the outline of his sword, suddenly bathed in a pale green light.

'Just die,' Luca snarled, and the green light pulsed like a heartbeat.

Luca gasped. He reached for his own sword. It was painfully cold, like an icicle against his skin. Carter was pressing a hand against his chest, and then so were the others. Only Freddie seemed unmoved by it. His face was white as marble, his eyes fixed on Luca.

'You made the swords go cold,' he said. 'Because of what you just said.'

And it seemed that the whole world was suddenly colder. Luca turned his face away from the sleet and snow.

'Don't hate,' Jess urged him.

'I don't know what to do...'

'Think of everything you love.'

Luca closed his eyes. He thought of his mum as he touched his sword's blade. The ice cold was gone. It felt different, almost asleep, waiting for him. Luca tried again to think of good things, but it was too hard. All he could think of was Madoc's grinning face, that horrible black sword hanging around his neck and how he wanted to destroy both. In one moment of absolute clarity, he understood.

Madoc's sword needs evil and hatred. Ours need love.

Luca stood up. There was no time left. It was now or never. Madoc was winning. Luca pulled his sword out of his shirt and held it up. The blade was dull. He stared at it, willing it to come alive, but nothing happened. He shook the damn thing, swearing and cursing it.

'That won't work. Ignore the sword. Look at me.'

Jess was next to him. Her arms wrapped him up.

'That's it. Focus on me. Focus on what we all mean to each other. When we stood over the raven there was so much love. We can do that again.'

'But the raven's dying. We didn't do anything.'

'Yes, we did.'

Jess smiled at him, almost willing him to understand. She hugged him even more tightly, and he hoped she would never let go.

Something made Luca look up at the Tower. A dense black cloud had gathered over them, swirling in strange patterns, breaking and forming. He felt it then. He knew what was coming.

'Too late, boy,' Madoc shouted. 'You're too late!'

Gwen raised up her sword and thrust it at her father.

'I don't think so.'

Madoc's mouth fell open.

'You've got one...you can't have one...how?'

'Mum,' Gwen replied. 'Understand now?'

'But you're a Madoc.'

'And a Plantagenet. So you can choke on it. These are my friends. You're nothing.'

'It's Bran,' said Freddie calmly. 'Look over there.'

The children turned as one. A black shape glided down. Luca felt his heart leap. It *was* Bran. The cloud broke apart into thousands of birds, their voices rising in a terrible scream that was louder than the wind. Luca didn't think he'd ever heard anything so beautiful in all his life.

'Bran!' He shouted as the raven landed on the Tower walls.

'Shoot it!' Madoc screamed.

His men emptied their weapons. Then the gunfire stopped, and through the smoke Luca saw that Bran was untouched. He was standing atop the White Tower. His wings were outstretched and he called out loudly, over and over again.

Madoc's face curled into a mask of rage. He grabbed Madeleine by the shoulders.

'Kill this one. Then the others. Kill them all!'

Hug-a-Bug fell face down into a puddle.

'She's just a kid,' Luca said. 'Let her go.'

Madoc just smiled. 'Make me.'

A noise like a rushing train was building in Luca's head. He ran forwards, unstoppable and beyond control. Something was happening to him. His legs had strength they shouldn't have. His skin shimmered and changed.

'Bloody hell,' Carter shouted. 'It's like what Peake did. Luca can do it as well!'

Luca was no longer a boy. Luca was a lion, too far gone in his rage to really understand. He was now more animal than human, claws and teeth ready to attack. Madoc was struck dumb with fear, an easy target. His terror filled Luca's nostrils, a thousand times stronger than any human could ever smell. Luca leaped. He was ready to kill.

'No!'

Gwen's shout cut through his animal senses. He twisted and landed clumsily, and the rage faded just enough for Luca to remember who he was.

I'm better than him, he thought. I won't become the same.

The lion was gone. He was Luca again, but it was too late to stop. He barrelled into Madoc, knocking him backwards over the edge of the path towards the Thames. Luca instinctively grabbed Madoc's hand, then a shoulder. His brain whirled at the madness of it. What had just happened to him?

Madoc's eyes locked on Luca's, full of hatred and fear. The river surged twenty metres beneath him, a grey ribbon of death.

'You changed,' he gasped. 'I saw it but I don't believe it. What was that...that thing?'

'Just don't let go if you want to live.'

'Live? After you've taken everything from me?'

'Pull yourself up, Madoc. I can't hold on for much longer.'

'So now you're going to save me and be the hero.'

Luca's hand slipped.

'Not a hero, Madoc. Just what any normal person would do.'

Sweat bubbled up on Luca's face. The muscles and tendons burned with the effort. Madoc looked down at the swirling waters.

'I won't let you fall!' Luca shouted.

'And I won't let you save me.'

Luca saw a streak of green light, then a sickening pain exploded in his hand as Madoc slipped away. Luca held his hand against his chest, the hot blood spreading across his jacket. He looked at the wound where Madoc had stabbed him. It was small, no bigger than a penny, but the pain was building into something so awful he wanted to scream. His fingers opened and closed. His whole arm shook.

The   black   skull...black   skull...
evil...hate...anger...evil...hate...hate...hate...

Luca's head was filled with all the voices of the Madocs down the years, and he knew it was going to drive him as mad as them. A shadow passed over him. He looked up, his vision blurred with hot tears. Jess was touching his face, his hair, his arm.

'I love you,' she whispered.

She stroked his hand, her fingers against the stab wound. The pain eased. The voices faded from his mind. They were surrounded by ravens. He felt light, almost floating. He tried to smile, to speak, to tell his friends he was okay, but they were disappearing into the blackness. He was off the ground, carried on the birds' wings. He relaxed, hoping the others were coming with him. The rain faded into nothing. The wind dropped away. All he could hear was the rhythmic beating of wings and a soft voice whispering his name.

'Is that you, Bran?'

You called, Pendragon. We came.

44

A cold sun hung low in a darkening sky. Frost covered the lawns and gravel. There was barely enough wind to move the flag on top of the white Tower. It was a strange stillness, as if something terrible had been there and then moved on, leaving the faintest trace of itself behind, like an old memory or a half remembered dream.

'We did it,' Luca said, rubbing his bandaged leg.

'You did,' the Ravenmaster replied. 'And leave that alone. It'll start bleeding again.'

Thousands of ravens covered the walls and lawns of the Tower, all sat silently staring at Luca like soldiers waiting for orders.

'You're definitely the boss around here, son. And I hope they're not all planning on stopping. I've only got room for seven.'

'I still don't understand most of this.'

'Maybe you're not supposed to. Not yet, anyway.'

'Maybe. I'm sorry about Morgan and Jarvis.'

'So am I. They knew the risks. It's a military thing.'

'Like my dad.'

'Yeah. Like your dad.'

Madeleine was running towards them. She was dirty and her hair was a wild tangle but her eyes were shining with pure joy.

'I love all the ravens,' she shouted. 'And they love me. I want to go flying again. I want them to carry me to the moon.'

'Special kid,' McKenna said.

'She so is.'

Madeleine threw her arms around her uncle.

'I wish we could have saved the final raven. He was nice, like Hug-a-Bug. I wanted to love him better.'

'I think you loved him plenty,' Luca said. 'You loved him enough to bring all his friends here.'

McKenna gave Luca a huge smile as he hugged his niece.

'You did that, my darling. All of you did.'

'We got rid of the bad men. The ravens dropped them in the river.' Her face darkened. 'I think they all drowned.'

'Maybe they did. Don't think about it any more. Now come with me. Let's go and ring your dad and tell him all about it. I bet he's already hard at work finding a way to fix the virus.'

Luca watched them walk away, hand in hand.

What I would give now to be able to make a call like that, he thought.

'He'd be very proud.'

He turned to Jess, silent and unnoticed.

'You reading my thoughts?'

'Sorry. That one was too loud to miss. And it's true, Luca. Your dad would be so proud of everything you've done.'

Luca blushed and looked away.

'You said something to me...did you mean it?'

It was Jess's turn to blush. They sat in awkward silence, listening to the soft rustle of the trees and the murmuring of the ravens around them.

'Say something, Jess. Anything.'

'I meant it.'

Luca swallowed hard.

'I love you too.'

She took his hand. He enjoyed the feel of her cool skin, the way their fingers locked together.

'I made you a promise,' he said.

'You kept it. You helped me get Freddie back.'

'I couldn't have done that without you. Or the others. We're...like a team, or something.'

'Children of Camelot, Peake called us.'

'I want to go home and see my mum.'

'And I want to see my baby brother.'

She leaned against him. They watched the surviving Warders clear up the signs of battle – the discarded weapons, the random splashes of blood. Freddie walked past, his hands full of spent cartridges. He didn't look at them and his face gave nothing away.

'Freddie will probably have lots to say about you and me. He can get a bit jealous.'

'As long as we give him enough chocolate, we should be okay.'

They both laughed, and it felt good. Carter and Gwen were approaching.

'All right, you two?'

Carter was grinning, nodding at their hands.

'Interrupting anything?'

'Leave them alone, you idiot,' said Gwen, punching his shoulder. She crouched down in front of Luca. 'Are you all right? That was a bit intense.'

'I think so. Yes. Look, Gwen...I...'

'I know you tried to save him.'

'I was ready to kill him, not save him.'

'But you didn't. The real you came back. The Luca we all know.'

'Cool trick with the lion thing, though,' Carter added. 'Any idea how you did it?'

'None at all.'

'Shame. Anyway, we should get out of here before people turn up and start asking awkward questions.'

'Where would we go?'

'Carter and I have talked it through,' Gwen said. 'I need to go back to Lundy.'

'Of course,' Jess replied. 'And I think you'll be welcome.'

'I hope so. What about you?'

'I want to see my brother. And Luca his mum.'

Gwen nodded.

'Your dad might have survived,' Luca said.

'I hope he didn't.'

Before he could answer, a whoosh of warm air swept through his hair.

'Bran!' Luca said as the raven settled onto his shoulder. 'You came for us!'

Bran pecked at his ears. He rubbed his beak against Luca's chest.

'Get off, you big lump,' he laughed, his heart bursting with unexpected love for the strange old bird.

Bran's eyes twinkled, but only for a moment. A great rumble began from somewhere beneath the White Tower. The ground shook. Freddie stopped what he was doing. He stood rigid, the bullet cases tumbling from his hands. He turned like a robot, his eyes black and glaring.

'At last,' a ghostly voice said from somewhere inside him.

Gwen's sword flicked out from her neck like a dog chasing a ball.

'I see my sword found its way to the Tower,' Freddie continued in his new strange voice. 'And my descendent is a girl. Your world must be a strange place.'

Freddie looked directly at Luca.

'You *must* find and release me. I have been a prisoner for too long!'

Then Freddie jolted upright. His arms thrashed as if he was fighting someone, or something. He closed his eyes. When they opened, the blackness was gone.

'That was the Black Prince,' Freddie said. 'We should probably do as he says.'

45

Canterbury - February.

The old man shook his head, trying to clear his mind. He staggered to his feet. He didn't know where he was. He didn't know how he had got here. All he knew was that everything hurt and that he was freezing cold.

He rubbed his temples, desperate to find a way into the maze of his memory. There were some faces and then they were gone in an instant, but they were the first real things he had been able to focus on since he had woken up in this unfamiliar place.

He scrunched his eyes tightly shut, hoping the faces would come back. He didn't have long to wait. They came in a tidal wave - shouting, smiling, laughing, leering, snarling, spitting and screaming, a few thousand years of memories.

The man slumped back against the damp stone wall of the cathedral. It was as if a bomb had exploded in his brain. Then it all faded away, leaving something new. He had knowledge and understanding of what he was.

Now, I just need my name. Without a name, what am I? No more than a rabbit in a field, or a worm underground.

The day was coming to life. He lowered his head as a couple walked past but they didn't notice him. He stared at an insignificant lump of rock just ahead of him, almost completely buried beneath the patchy grass. A memory of a long time before came back to him.

This is where Arthur pulled the sword from the stone, he thought.

He was surprised at how clearly it came to him.

Yes, this is the place. Canterbury.

He kneeled down and laid both hands on the rock, enjoying the feel of the mosses and lichens under his fingertips. He searched for a slim break in the surface where a blade might have once entered, but the years had closed over the hole.

I was Merlin.

The name jolted him. His mind began to focus, pulling together the strands of memories like braids of a rope.

The last name I had...what was it?

He balled his fist and banged it against his forehead. How could the most recent name be the most difficult to remember?

Poke? Something like that. Pike...pork? No, that's a stupid idea. Come on, think. Paint... pea...peak...Peake!

'My name was Peake,' he said, in a voice he didn't recognise, because it came from a different throat, from different lungs, through a different mouth.

He headed into the town, repeating the name over and over, muttering it in a hundred different languages and accents. He paused by a brightly lit shop window. The reflection revealed a man who was tall and slim with high cheekbones and sandy hair, grey at the temples. The nose was prominent, almost hawk-like. The eyes were deep green.

'I'm not Peake any more,' muttered the man. 'He's gone. Who am I now?'

Ambrose, he suddenly thought. That's my new name.

He pushed up the sleeve of his coat, knowing the tattoo would be there, no matter how many times his body changed.

'I showed them the bear,' Ambrose said, and another flurry of recent memories came back. He was on the causeway, fighting. He was a wolf. An eagle. A dragon...

He closed his eyes and let his mind wander. He searched for their thoughts and their voices. It took a while, but he found them. He saw a boy and a girl with shining eyes sitting on a hospital bed. A younger child was laughing. He took the chocolate offered to him by his brother. The youngster had a drip in one arm but the man didn't sense any illness in him. He was going to live.

He moved on – a boy stood beside a canal, staring into the water. A girl approached, tall and beautiful. They hugged and walked away, holding hands.

Then he found himself in a brightly lit laboratory. A man was checking an endless list of numbers on a screen. He was smiling at his daughter. Her red hair shone under the lights. She was playing with a dirty old stuffed ladybird.

Ambrose blinked and everything changed again. He was in a tiny room. The electric fire gave off a welcoming glow. A woman held a tattered photograph of a soldier and a young boy. She was smiling.

'She's alive, Luca,' he whispered. 'And you saved her.'

His mind was searching again. He was somewhere dark and terrifying – there was a man under water, struggling to breathe. His arms flailed and his legs kicked until he broke through the surface of a filthy river and flopped onto a clay bank. The man looked up. The sky was full of ravens.

So Madoc survived, he thought. Of course.

The images faded away. He glanced back at the shop window. A television at the back of the shop caught his attention. He watched the silent images of the Prime Minister addressing Parliament. Text scrolled along the screen.

...BREAKING NEWS...FLU UNDER CONTROL, SAY EXPERTS AT GOVERNMENT LABORATORY...VACCINE WORKING...JOHN MADOC STILL MISSING IN WRECKAGE OF THE SHARD...

'Are you okay, sir?'

Ambrose turned to face a boy of about fourteen. He wore an unusual wing collared shirt. His tie flew off to one side and his hair hadn't seen a comb in a while. The boy was tall for his age, with a thin face.

'Fine, thank you.'

'You were talking to yourself, that's all,' the boy continued. 'I wondered if you were all right.'

The man nodded.

'I'm fine, thank you.'

They stood in silence for a few moments. Then the boy spoke.

'If you don't mind, I have to go. I'm late for lessons.' He started to walk away, then turned. 'I feel as if I know you.'

'I suppose I might be a friend of your father,' the man said.

The boy's eyes darkened.

'No. My father died when I was very young.'

'I'm sorry to hear that,' the man replied, understanding more with every second that passed. 'My name's Ambrose, by the way.'

'Pleased to meet you, Mr Ambrose,' the boy replied, then he continued on his way.

Ambrose watched him pass through an ancient archway and head towards his school. A harsh croak sounded out from somewhere nearby. Ambrose smiled as a raven settled onto his shoulder.

'Hello Bran. Another new face and name, I'm afraid.'

He glanced back at the archway where the boy's footsteps echoed off the road.

'And I'm pleased to meet you too, George Randall,' he whispered. 'I expect we'll be seeing each other again very soon.'

ACKNOWLEDGEMENTS

Thanks go to:

Mum and Dad - for a house full of books. Ken Allen - for letting me take whatever I wanted from Beech Books. John & Lisa McKenna, Charlie & Toby Quartley, Pete & Emma Tebbutt – for your patience above and beyond the call of duty, and for being the best mates in the world. Ben Illis – for telling me I could write and helping me connect with some great people. Lu Hersey – your help made the difference when the whole thing was a mess. Liz Flanagan – for being an editor guru with wise words and a route out of draft hell. Helen Dennis – for your boundless enthusiasm and positivity. I don't know when you find time to breathe! Adele & Jim Parks – for a wonderful friendship over so many years, and for your unshakeable support. Freddie Quartley – sorry it took so long! Sam McKenna – for not being able to sleep until you had finished the book, and for lending me your name! Doug & Cara Scally – thanks for reading and enjoying one of the many versions. Damian & Amanda Scally – for friendship and never being afraid to ask 'how's it going'! Imogen Cooper, Ness Harbour and the Golden Egg Academy – you are an amazing bunch of people and I'm so humbled to have been a small part of it all. Simon Hall – for constant Twitter support and the best workshop at the Winchester Writers' Conference. Martin Griffin – for talking it all through and for loving the book. I owe you, mate. Madeleine and George – you're the most amazing kids. I'm so proud of you and I love you so much. Jo & Barry Smith – for love, friendship and belief. Without you, it would never have happened. Thank you beyond words. Sara – you inspire me every day. I love you more than you'll ever know. You never stopped believing it would happen. We did it.